THE SHY ONE

THE SHY ONE

Dorothy sat on the porch steps and stared up at the sky.
Suddenly she saw a single star, the first star of evening.
She clasped her hands and softly chanted:

> "Star light, star bright
> First star I see tonight.
> Wish I may, wish I might
> Have the wish I wish tonight."

She waited a long time, going over in her mind all
the things she might wish for. Then, from within the
deepest layers of her heart, Dorothy wished to stop
being shy.

THE SHY ONE

BY DOROTHY NATHAN

ILLUSTRATED BY CAROLYN CATHER

SCHOLASTIC BOOK SERVICES
NEW YORK · TORONTO · LONDON · AUCKLAND · SYDNEY

Copyright © 1966 by Dorothy Nathan. This edition is published by Scholastic Book Services, a division of Scholastic Magazines, Inc., by arrangement with Random House, Inc.

2nd printing............December 1971

Printed in the U.S.A.

*Dedicated to the shy ones
who may read this book*

CONTENTS

CHAPTER ONE

Dorothy Makes a Wish

Dorothy loved to greet her father when he came home from work. Tonight she was setting the table for supper when she heard the telltale creak of the front gate. She threw down a handful of forks and raced through the house. Out the front door, down the path and into Daddy's out-stretched arms.

Daddy rubbed his prickly cheek against her smooth one. "How's my oldest daughter this evening?" he asked.

But before Dorothy had time to say a word, her eight-year-old sister Anabelle bounded out of the house and hurtled herself at Daddy, too.

"Watch out!" said Daddy. "One of these days you two are going to knock me right off my feet!"

He chucked Anabelle's chin and kissed her forehead and started slowly toward the house, a girl tucked under either arm. Right under the apple tree, he stopped. "By the way, do you girls remember that Sunday is Mama's birthday?"

They nodded. Anabelle said, "We've talked about it lots of times."

"Had any ideas about a present?"

"I think she'd like a fern," said Dorothy. "You know, to go in the parlor window where the rubber plant died? Only I'm afraid a fern is too expensive."

"Well, I have eleven cents," said Anabelle. "I'll give all of it. Wait a minute!" She darted into the house—Anabelle never walked if she could run—and returned swinging one of her long black cotton stockings. Coins jingled in the toe.

At this moment Mama appeared at the front door. "Hello, dear," she said to Daddy. "I thought I heard your voice."

"We'll have to talk about this later," Daddy whispered to the girls, and he went on into the house.

Dorothy and Anabelle lingered on the front path. It was an interesting path because it was paved in cement that was full of cracks, and these cracks took the shapes of bears or elephants if you looked at them the right way. But now the girls were not studying cracks.

"When are we going to make Mama's May baskets?" Anabelle asked. "It's already Thursday."

"I've been thinking about May baskets." Dorothy swung herself back and forth from the lowest limb of the apple tree. The tree was thick with young blue-green leaves and tightly folded, pink-tipped buds. "And I think maybe this year we should skip the baskets."

"Oh, no!" Anabelle cried out. "We've just got to have them. Mama's birthday wouldn't be right without May baskets. Please, Dorothy, let's make baskets!"

"Well . . ." said Dorothy, swinging. She hoped Anabelle would go on urging. Every year since they could remember, the girls had woven May baskets from strips of bright-colored drawing paper. They filled the baskets with flowers and surprised Mama on her birthday, which fell on May the first. Dorothy had always enjoyed the game, but this year she wasn't sure whether to go on with it. After all, she was almost eleven now, and May baskets were pretty childish.

"Please?" wheedled Anabelle. "Pretty please with honey on it?"

"Girls!" Mama called from the kitchen door. "Suppertime!"

"Well . . ." Dorothy said, letting go of the tree, still pretending to be reluctant. "Will you wipe the dishes next time it's my turn?"

"Yes," said Anabelle. "If you'll help me make my handle. Handles are hard."

"All right." Happy to have been talked into making May baskets after all, Dorothy took her sister's hand. They walked slowly around to the back door.

The girls lived in a white shingled house in the tiny town of Woodburn, Oregon. Woodburn had one paved road, Main Street, and a business district three blocks long. Daddy's hardware store was right across from the railway station. Trains roared past all day long but they seldom stopped in Woodburn.

Most of the farmers in the area still drove horse and buggies. But by now, 1921, more and more people were buying automobiles. Daddy yearned to own one, but Mama and Dorothy were rather afraid of them. Automobiles whizzed along so fast, sometimes at as much as twenty miles an hour. And the dust they stirred up!

Anabelle opened the back door. Dorothy followed her sister through the pantry and into the big, warm kitchen. Mama was ladling noodle soup into bowls. Daddy was already seated at the table with an open letter in front of him.

Dorothy glanced at the letter. As usual, it was written in Russian, or else Yiddish. She didn't know which and couldn't tell one from the other. Mama and Daddy had been receiving a lot of these letters lately. Dorothy knew they came from relatives who lived in Russia, but they didn't interest her much. She had never met any relatives, and Russia was very far away.

"Wash your hands, girls. And please do a good job, I don't want streaks on my clean towel." Mama's words were normal, but her tone of voice was not. It sounded high and excited.

Dorothy looked at her mother. Mama's eyes were blue or gray or green, depending on her mood. Right now her eyes were a shining blue and there were splashes of high color on her cheeks.

"What's happened?" asked Dorothy, looking from one parent to the other. "Is something the matter?"

"Nothing is wrong." Mama put the last of the steaming bowls on the table and sat down at her place. "We've had some exciting news. Sit down and drink your soup, girls, before it gets cold, and Daddy will tell you about it."

Dorothy hastily wet the palms of her hands and waved them in the general direction of the soap dish. She blotted them on the roller towel and quickly took her seat at the table.

But Daddy was well into his own soup before, at last, he put down his spoon. "I've told you girls many times about how the Jews were persecuted in Russia," he began.

Dorothy nodded.

"And about how thousands of Jews left Russia to go to friendlier countries—to England and France and Palestine——"

"And, best of all, to America," Mama interrupted. "Thank God your daddy and I were fortunate enough to come to America."

Dorothy thanked God, too. She couldn't imagine being anything but an American.

"When your mama and I first came to live in Woodburn," said Daddy, finishing his soup, "we expected to help the rest of our family get here, too. But times changed—there was the great war in Europe and nobody could get out of Russia any more."

"I know," said Dorothy, as her mother collected the empty soup bowls. "And we have one grandma and Uncle Max still living there."

Mama set an enormous platter of chicken stew in the middle of the oilcloth-covered table.

"That's where you're wrong," said Daddy, helping himself to a chicken leg and some potatoes and carrots. "Grandma and Uncle Max are *not* in Russia. Not any more. They're in New York City this very minute."

"Goody!" Anabelle bounced up and down in her chair.

"How did they get out of Russia?" Dorothy took a bite of white meat from the chicken breast, her favorite part. "You told us nobody could get in or out of Russia."

"They escaped," said Daddy. "They sneaked out one dark night, leaving their house all lit up as though everything was just as usual."

Dorothy and Anabelle were wide-eyed. This was as exciting as an adventure story.

"Your Uncle Max hid a rowboat under the bushes at the edge of the Black Sea, just outside their village," Daddy continued. "And one night, when the coast was clear, he and your grandmother left. They tiptoed out with nothing but the clothes on their backs."

"Then what?" asked Anabelle.

"They got into the rowboat and Uncle Max rowed out into the Black Sea. It was six days before a ship picked them up. An English wheat freighter, going to Liverpool. Your Uncle Max is a brave boy. Not many fourteen-year-old boys could do what he did!"

"How did Grandma and Uncle Max live for six days in a rowboat? What did they have to eat?

How come they didn't die of thirst?" Dorothy had just finished reading *Robinson Crusoe*, all about a shipwrecked adventurer. This story was every bit as good. Better, because these were her very own relatives.

"Those are fine questions, Dorothy. You can ask Uncle Max when you see him next week."

Dorothy felt the blood pound up into her face. "When I *see* him? Next *week*?"

"Is he coming here?" squealed Anabelle.

Daddy picked up the letter. "I wasn't sure of it until this afternoon," he said, "but they're in New York now. It will only take them another five days and five nights to cross the United States. Next Tuesday we'll meet their train in Portland. And by Tuesday night, if God is willing, Grandma and Uncle Max will be safely home in Woodburn with us."

Anabelle got up and danced around the table, hooting with excitement.

Mama wiped her eyes on a corner of her apron and said, "After twelve years of struggling and praying! At least these two are saved!"

But Dorothy—Dorothy's throat closed as it always did when she was upset. She put down her fork. She would choke if she ate another bite.

"Finish your supper, dear," said Mama.

"Why does my news upset you?" Daddy frowned a little as he slipped two lumps of sugar into his glass of hot tea. "I thought you'd be happy to welcome your relatives. They are the only grandma and the only uncle you have."

"I'm happy!" Anabelle piped up.

"Shh." Mama patted Daddy's sleeve. "Leave her alone. After Dorothy gets to know them she won't feel so shy. You know how fearful she's always been with strangers."

"I am *not* shy! I am *not* afraid!" Dorothy pushed back her chair, fighting the tears that were rising in her voice. "It's just—" She cast about for some reason, any reason. "It's just that there isn't any room in this house for more people!"

She threw her napkin on the table and rushed from the room. Through the living room and out the front hall. Slam! went the door.

Outside, a soft April twilight was gathering. Dorothy stood on the porch, breathing in calmness with the clean apple-blossom air. At length she sat down on the top step and stared up at the sky, trying to swallow away the lump in her throat. It wouldn't go. Her throat throbbed with the weight of things she couldn't seem to help.

After a while the front door opened and Anabelle came out. "You missed rice pudding for dessert," she said, sitting down at the far end of Dorothy's step. "With raisins and hazelnuts in it. Yum." Anabelle rubbed her stomach and rolled her eyes to express her opinion of the pudding.

Mama and Daddy came onto the porch, Daddy carrying his unfinished glass of tea. They settled themselves into a pair of wicker rocking chairs. The chairs creaked back and forth while Daddy sipped his tea. At length he said in a gentle voice, "Of course you're right, Dorothy. We will be crowded here with six people."

"We thought you girls would double up in Dorothy's room," said Mama. "So Grandma can use Anabelle's. Max will just have to sleep on the parlor sofa for the time being."

"I expect it will only be a temporary arrangement," said Daddy.

He seemed about to continue. But Mama, looking at Dorothy's face, said, "Enough for now, Avram. It's too much for children to understand at one time." She stood and took a deep breath. "Come, let's all go for a walk. This air is delicious."

Anabelle, ever ready, jumped up from her step. Daddy set his empty tea glass on top of the wide porch rail. But Dorothy shook her head. She felt as though she had a throat full of gravel.

Daddy offered one arm to Mama and the other to Anabelle. Dorothy watched her family stroll off down the block. Her elbows were on her knees and her cheeks rested on the tips of her index fingers. She often sat this way in the hope of making dimples in her cheeks.

Dorothy closed her eyes and began a list of the things she was afraid of: Dogs if they were barky. Automobiles because they went so fast. Boys, always so sure of themselves. Strange grownups. Knocking at neighbors' doors to ask for old newspapers for the school's paper drive. And now these new relatives.

Too many things! Why wasn't she born easy and friendly, like Anabelle? A long time ago, Dorothy used to cling to Mama's skirt whenever a stranger was around. Of course she was only a little girl then. Mama's friends always said she'd outgrow it.

And she did outgrow it, Dorothy told herself. Nowadays she wouldn't dream of hanging on to Mama, no matter how much she wanted to hide.

Dorothy sat bolt upright. If she really, really tried, could she somehow get over that feeling of needing to hide? Maybe it would be nice to have an Uncle Max. Certainly no dog would jump on her when Uncle Max was around. He might play with her, even teach her how to ride a bicycle. . . .

Suddenly Dorothy saw, floating in the blueness above her head, a yellow slice of new moon. One single star lay cradled in the curve of the moon.

Dorothy was positive there had been no moon, no star, last time she looked up at the sky. She stared hard at the star and the star sparkled and glittered back at her. Dorothy clasped her hands and softly chanted:

> "Star light, star bright
> First star I see tonight.
> Wish I may, wish I might
> Have the wish I wish tonight."

She waited a long time, going over in her mind all the things she might wish for. Then, from within the deepest layers of her heart, Dorothy wished to stop being shy.

CHAPTER TWO

The Hiding Place

Next morning Dorothy woke up with a funny hot feeling in her throat. After breakfast, Mama asked her to stand in the light and stick out her tongue. With a firm hand on Dorothy's chin, Mama peered inside and tried to decide which ailment this one was. It could be the kind of sore throat Mama couldn't treat—the misery that rose and fell like a thermometer of Dorothy's feelings. On the other hand, Dorothy might be coming down with a cold and a runny nose.

"Better play safe and stay home from school today," Mama decided. "Climb on this stool, Anabelle, so I can comb your hair."

With expert fingers Mama brushed Anabelle's reddish hair into ringlets. She fastened a white taffeta hair ribbon on top and glanced at the kitchen clock on the wall next to the big iron stove. The clock's long brass pendulum ticked briskly back and forth. Both hands now stood on the gold Roman numeral IX.

"Quarter to nine already!" Mama exclaimed. "Time for you to run along, dear." She kissed Anabelle good-by and began to wash the breakfast dishes.

Behind Mama's back, Anabelle whispered to Dorothy, "When will we start making the baskets?"

"Today. This afternoon," Dorothy whispered back.

"Dorothy, keep away from your sister," warned Mama, who often claimed she had eyes in the back of her head. "If you're coming down with a cold I don't want Anabelle to catch it. Anabelle, you'll be late if you don't leave this minute. And remember to take your lunch."

Anabelle picked up a brown paper bag from the table, waved her final good-by and dashed out. Dorothy stood at a kitchen window and watched until her little sister had disappeared around the corner. Dorothy could tell that Anabelle felt important because she was going to school today while Dorothy stayed home.

In her mind, Dorothy heard the jangle of the school bell. She imagined Miss Cole, the principal, standing on the top step with the brass bell in her hand.

The children would be lining up outside the building, first the girls and then the boys. Now they were marching in. When the last boy was safely inside the hall, Miss Cole would close the heavy oak door, shutting out the rest of the world.

Suddenly Dorothy felt very much alone. If she hurried, maybe she could still get to school before the bell rang. . . .

"Dorothy, please come over to the sink so I can fix you up."

Dorothy sighed as she obeyed. Mama's way of treating a sore throat made life difficult. First she dipped a linen tea towel in cold water and squeezed it dry. Then she folded the towel into a long thin strip and wrapped the clammy thing around Dorothy's neck. After that, to keep Dorothy from catching cold, Mama wound a dry Turkish towel over the damp linen one. Finally, she fastened the whole clumsy bandage onto itself with two large safety pins.

"There you are," said Mama. "Keep out of drafts." She hurried upstairs to make the beds.

Suddenly the morning stretched ahead of Dorothy, empty. It was a beautiful Friday in April. But with her neck in prison, what was there for a girl to do?

Dorothy drifted back to the window, feeling aimless. If she were at school, she might be coloring pictures of elegant kimono-clad ladies, to paste in her report about Japan.

But no, today was Friday. That meant she would be bringing her weekly paper-drive report up to date. She would add the latest figures and write them on the blackboard in red and yellow chalk. Since the beginning of the month, Woodburn Elementary School pupils had been competing fiercely in a paper drive. The class bringing in the most paper by the time the drive ended would win a prize.

Dorothy pressed her forehead against the window glass and imagined herself turning in bundles and bundles of newspapers. How pleased her teacher would be! How surprised the other pupils in Mrs. Merrick's class! Dorothy could just hear Enid Stidd ask in amazement, "Where did you get all that paper?"

Dorothy smiled and tossed her head as she answered, "Oh, I rode all over Woodburn on my bicycle, knocking at everybody's door. It was easy."

The telephone cleared its throat with a "cling" that meant in a few seconds it was going to ring. The little noise ended Dorothy's daydream. In truth she had turned in only a measly ten pounds of paper so far, Daddy's old *Portland Oregonians*. And even if she owned a bicycle and knew how to ride it (which she didn't) she would never find the nerve to go about asking strangers for their magazines and papers. Or speak so freely to Enid Stidd, either. Enid Stidd was the most popular girl in the fifth grade and Dorothy seldom said a word to her.

Now the telephone did ring, two longs and a short: R–i–n–g! R–i–n–g! Ring!

"Will you answer the phone for me, please?" Mama called over the banister.

Dorothy hurried to the little table where the telephone stood on one of Mama's embroidered lace doilies. The instrument had a long dark stem with a shiny metal mouthpiece at the top. It looked like a black and silver daffodil.

Mama came clattering down the stairs as Dorothy lifted the receiver from its hook. "Hello?"

"Hello? Hello?" It was Miss Susie Michaels,

Dorothy's piano teacher. "Dorothy? What are you doing at home this time of the morning?"

"Here's Mama," said Dorothy, surrendering the receiver to her mother. She stood by to listen. Her heart beat fast with hope that Miss Michaels was calling to cancel today's piano lesson.

Mama's end of the conversation was not revealing. "Nothing much, just a little sore throat." Pause. "Of course you can. Certainly." Longer pause. "Well, I'll be glad to hear about it. We'll see you shortly. Good-by."

Before Mama had the receiver back on its hook Dorothy asked, "Is Miss Michaels too sick to come today?"

Mama smiled. "She's not at all sick. She called to cancel the lesson because she has to go to Portland this afternoon. But when she found you were home this morning she said she would come and give you a lesson now."

Dorothy groaned. She hated practicing half an hour every day. She hated trying to figure out the bass notes for the left hand. In fact, she hated piano lessons.

"Do I *have* to take a lesson today? Even with my sore throat?" Dorothy put a hand on her bandaged neck.

"You know you aren't really sick," said Mama, testing Dorothy's forehead with the palm of her hand. "Just a little sore throat."

Dorothy frowned and tried to look feverish. She wished for a truly fancy illness—diphtheria or influenza or perhaps the black plague. Anything to protect her from Miss Michaels.

"Anabelle doesn't take piano lessons, so why do I have to?"

"Your sister isn't old enough yet," said Mama patiently. "I've told you a hundred times, when she's your age Anabelle will study violin. Every well-brought-up young lady should know how to play some instrument. Now that's enough arguing, I haven't time for it." Mama twisted a loose curl around a long brown hairpin and stuck it firmly back into the bun on her neck. "Cheer up, Miss Michaels says she has a surprise for us."

"What is it?"

"I don't know yet. Come along, you can help me in the kitchen until she gets here."

Mama hurried into the kitchen with Dorothy at her heels. "Bring out the yellow mixing bowl," she instructed as she poked the fire in the stove. "We'll start a cake first, and then I'll set my bread. Be careful of that bowl. I brought it with me from Russia."

Dorothy trotted into the pantry and lifted the heavy mixing bowl from its place on the shelf. It was a creamy yellow, with three bands of blue near the rim for decoration. The pottery was coarse but the bowl was a cheerful round shape and the most delicious cakes came out of it.

"Thank you," said Mama, who was piling kindling and lumps of coal into the stove. "Now ten eggs, please."

Dorothy walked to the cooler, which was really a cupboard against the outside wall of the house. There were openings at the back of the cooler, covered with fine wire screening to let air in and keep bugs out.

She carried the eggs over to the wooden drainboard. While she broke them into the bowl, Mama added a wedge of butter and measured out the sugar and the flour. Then Mama sat down by the kitchen table. She held the bowl securely in her apron-covered lap while she creamed eggs and butter together with a long-handled wooden mixing spoon. Dorothy stood by and waited with the cup of sugar. Whenever Mama nodded, Dorothy poured a little sugar into the bowl and watched it swirl into the mixture and gradually get lost.

After the flour and vanilla and buttermilk were all beaten in, Mama poured the thick yellow batter into tins and set the tins gently into the hot oven.

"Now for the bread," said Mama. Her shoes clicked over the linoleum floor as she hurried about, assembling ingredients and utensils. She hummed happily as she crumbled a soft cake of yeast into a small bowl of warm water. Mama always baked bread on Mondays and Fridays. She thought any housekeeper who used store-bought bread was a lazy, good-for-nothing woman.

"My heart is hurrying in my breast!" Mama burst out. "Just think, on Tuesday I'll see my mother again! I was a young bride when I kissed her last. And Max, my baby brother Max!"

Dorothy had never thought of her mother as ever having had a father and mother of her own. Now she imagined how it would be if she, Dorothy, didn't see Mama for twelve years. Longer than she'd even been alive! It was a horrible idea, and Dorothy got rid of it by hugging Mama around the waist with all her might. Mama, who was adding the dissolved yeast to a huge mound of dough, bent over and kissed the top of Dorothy's head.

"How will I talk to Grandma and Uncle Max?" asked Dorothy. "Can they speak English?"

"I don't know," said Mama. "Probably not very much." She placed the bread mixture in a large metal bucket with an arm made especially for kneading. "Here, Dorothy, you knead the bread so I can make an icing for the cake."

Dorothy stood near the mixing pail and turned the black-knobbed handle in an endless circle. The mixing arm went around and around inside.

"They must have learned a few words of English the two months they waited in Liverpool," said Mama. "At least Uncle Max must have. I'm not so sure about your grandma. It's harder for old people to learn new things, and she's had a terribly long, hard journey. I'm afraid your grandma is a very tired woman." Mama shook her head and looked worried.

When the dough was kneaded enough, Mama scraped the spongy mass onto the floured drainboard and cut it into six pieces. "Wash your hands if you want to handle the bread," she said.

Dorothy loved to work the good-smelling dough. Quickly she washed and dried her hands, and dusted them with flour so the bread wouldn't stick.

"What does Uncle Max look like?" she asked as she rolled and patted her piece of dough to form it into a loaf.

"I'm curious myself." Mama's expert fingers worked twice as fast as Dorothy's. "He was only two years old when I left. He was an adorable baby then, with black——"

There was a loud knock at the front door. "What, Miss Michaels already? I can't believe how the day is flying. Dorothy, will you let her in? I'm in flour up to my elbows."

Dorothy dragged herself slowly to the front door and opened it. Sure enough, there stood Miss Michaels in her rusty-green coat. Miss Michaels was a long thin lady with gray hair, who seemed to have more bones in her body than most people. She was rather deaf and talked in a loud voice.

"Well, good morning, Dorothy, and how are we?" Miss Michaels stepped inside and began to unfasten the lumpy buttons on her coat. "Did you practice faithfully for me this week? I have such a lovely surprise to share with you and your mama. Just wait till I tell you!" Miss Michaels hung up her coat and led the way into the parlor.

Dorothy followed, feeling no excitement about Miss Michaels' surprise. It would probably turn out to be just another new piece to practice.

Without thinking, Dorothy wrinkled her nose and flicked out her tongue behind Miss Michaels' stiffly corseted back. She knew she was being very rude but she couldn't help it. How she hated these Friday piano lessons!

CHAPTER THREE

"*Start with the Finger Exercises*"

"Start with the finger exercises." Miss Michaels patted the stool that stood in front of the shiny old upright piano. "When your fingers are warmed up I shall give you a new piece to work on."

Dorothy's fingers seemed to live a life of their own whenever she played the piano. Now they blundered up and down the keys trying to find the right notes for the A-minor scale. Miss Michaels listened with her head bent forward, one hand cupped behind her good ear. Now and then she made impatient noises with her tongue, and once she rapped Dorothy's knuckles with her pencil.

At last all the scales were finished. Miss Michaels leaned down to her shabby carpetbag and drew out a new score. "Here's a lovely little piece," she said, setting it on the music rack. "Let's see how well we can sight-read."

Dorothy stumbled slowly through the "Butter-fly Waltz." By the time she got to the final chord, the sheet of music was peppered with black pencil marks which Miss Michaels made to show Dorothy where she must be more careful.

Some half-hours were longer than others, Dorothy knew, but this lesson seemed to go on forever. At last Miss Michaels said, "All right, Dorothy, that will be all for today. I'll expect you to play this nicely by next Friday."

"Thank you, Miss Michaels," said Dorothy politely, edging her way out of the parlor.

But Miss Michaels said, "Don't go away yet, Dorothy. Don't you want to hear my surprise?"

Mother came out of the kitchen, wiping her hands on a towel.

"The reason I couldn't come to give you a lesson this afternoon is that I am going up to Portland," said Miss Michaels in an important voice. "And the reason I am going up to Portland is to arrange for the rental of a small recital hall in the Multnomah Hotel."

Trouble was coming. Dorothy felt a small flag of distress unfurl in her stomach. Portland was a big city, about thirty-five miles from Woodburn.

Dorothy had never been inside the Multnomah Hotel but she had seen it once or twice. It was an enormous building in a downtown of enormous buildings.

"Yes?" said Mama.

"I have decided to give my annual pupil recital in Portland this June. And Dorothy, you may be in it, performing the 'Butterfly Waltz.' But you shall have to study hard, my dear, and practice faithfully. Our recital is only six weeks off."

"No," said Dorothy. "I don't want to be in it."

"I think it would do her a world of good," said Miss Michaels, turning to Mama as though Dorothy had suddenly gone deaf. "Build up her self-confidence, you know."

Dorothy's insides were quaking. It was bad enough having to play the piano at all. The thought of sitting up there in front of a crowd of grown-up people—"No, I won't!"

"Think about it," coaxed Miss Michaels. "I have an idea it would please your mother very much."

"Indeed it would," said Mama. "How would it be if I made you a new dress? Just think how pretty you'd look in white organdy."

For a moment Dorothy didn't know what to do. Then she ran out of the parlor and up the stairs to her bedroom. She threw herself face down on her bed and felt around for old Raggedy Ann, whose home was on top of the pillow.

Raggedy Ann was a stuffed doll with yarn hair and shoe-button eyes. Her painted face was faded with age and hard use, and one leg was missing at the knee.

In spite of Raggedy Ann's misfortunes—maybe because of them—Dorothy loved her dearly. All her other dolls, with their pretty porcelain faces and stylish shoes, were abandoned now. They were stored away in boxes, or lay in untidy heaps on the floor of the closet. But Raggedy Ann held her place of honor. Dorothy didn't admit it, not even to Anabelle, but she still played with Raggedy Ann sometimes.

Dorothy hugged the doll for comfort and listened for sounds of Miss Michaels' leaving. Instead, the women's voices went into the kitchen. That meant Miss Michaels was staying for a cup of coffee and a slice of fresh-baked cake. Maybe they were planning to call her back downstairs and talk to her some more.

With Raggedy Ann held tight against her chest, Dorothy sneaked out into the hall and down the stairs. She opened the front door slowly, carefully, so that it did not give a single squeak. She closed it just as carefully behind her and tiptoed off the porch. She paused on the cracked front path and looked back at the long wooden porch with its white painted railing. Sunshine warmed the crown of Dorothy's head as she wondered where she could go to get away from Miss Michaels.

In summertime the porch would be completely shaded by morning glory vines. They ran up strings that Mama tied between the railing and ceiling. The area between porch and ground, a height of perhaps three feet, was covered with a wooden criss-cross lattice, painted green.

Now, in late April, the strings hung slack. There were no vines yet, and the lattice beneath the porch was bare. Dorothy noticed that one section stuck out the tiniest bit.

I wonder what's underneath? she thought, crouching near the lattice. She closed one eye and peered inside with the other. But she couldn't really see anything, just diamonds of sunlight across the dark earth. Maybe the lattice could come open a little.

Dorothy pried at the wood with her fingernails. It yielded a crack. She scratched some stones and soil out of the way. Now the section opened a few more inches. In fact, it was open wide enough, maybe, for her to s–q–u–e–e–z–e—yes, here she was!

She found herself perched midway in a long tunnel that stretched on either side of her the length of the porch. There wasn't room enough to stand, so Dorothy sat down on the edge of a jutting boulder.

The clip-clop of a horse's feet sounded in the distance. Dorothy quickly dragged the lattice closed. Nobody must notice this front door to her new hiding place! She peeked through one of the diamond-shaped openings to see who was passing by.

It turned out to be plump, white-haired Mr. Vancouver in striped overalls and a wide straw hat. Sitting alongside him on the buckboard was his black and tan beagle, Nipper. Mr. Vancouver was a farmer who lived a short distance outside of Woodburn. Dorothy knew him because he traded with Daddy. He was probably on his way down to Main Street right now, to buy something in Daddy's hardware store. Dorothy liked the pink-cheeked old man. The wrinkles in his face fell in kindly lines.

Only how could such a nice man own such a snappy dog? Once, a long time ago outside

Daddy's store, Dorothy had been bending to pet Nipper when he jumped up and bit her leg. From then on she had kept out of his way. Nipper was the right name for him, she thought.

Mr. Vancouver's horse and buggy disappeared from view, and the cloud of dust behind it settled back on the road. Dorothy's attention returned to her new hiding place. The hard-packed floor was criss-crossed with sunlight and gave off a most wonderful damp, earthy smell. What a glorious place and how lucky she was to have found it! She and Anabelle could make their May baskets here and Mama would never see a single tattletale scrap of paper.

Dorothy could hardly wait for Anabelle to get home from school. Maybe after supper tonight they could creep in here and tell each other ghost stories. Dorothy ran her fingers back and forth inside the towels on her neck, imagining how dark and scary this place would be at night. She shivered with pleasure.

When would Miss Michaels go home? Dorothy wished she had remembered to bring a book. The damp towels around her neck made her skin itch. Why not take them off? Her throat didn't hurt a bit. Dorothy unfastened the safety pins and unwound the towels. What a relief to feel the air on her moist neck.

At last the front door was opening. Footsteps sounded on the porch over Dorothy's head.

"Good-by!" said Mama.

"Good-by!" replied Miss Michaels. "I will see you next Friday."

Miss Michaels walked down the path to her car, a Model T Ford. She climbed up into the high, black tin lizzie, as Daddy called it, and started the

motor. The car roared and shook. It pulled slowly into the road and rattled off in a cloud of dust. Thank heavens, no more Miss Michaels.

But she'd be back next Friday. And what about the recital, would she make Dorothy be in the recital? No matter what happens, Dorothy thought, I won't do it.

Dorothy teetered on her rock, thinking of ways to avoid the recital. Possibly the piano would be stolen, so she couldn't practice. But that wasn't likely, because who would want a piano? Maybe she ought to break her arm? Ouch, no. All at once she knew what she'd do: she'd run away.

Dorothy closed her eyes as she made her plans. She would live in the woods outside of Woodburn, keeping alive on nuts and berries. She would not come home for years and years. Not until she was all grown up. When she finally did return she would find Mama sitting on the rocking chair out on the porch, her apron soggy with fallen tears. She would look up at Dorothy and ask weakly, "Who are you?"

"I am your daughter Dorothy. You drove me from home by being cruel. Aren't you sorry now?"

"Dorothy!" Mama got down on her knees. She looked up at Dorothy, hands clasped before her, and begged, "I wish I had never listened to Miss Michaels. Will you ever, ever forgive me? Please come home. I promise to throw the piano away."

"Of course I forgive you! Of course I'll come home!" The imaginary Mama was so pitiful that real tears sprang into Dorothy's eyes. She opened them and her daydream ended. Running away was no good. She couldn't let Mama be so unhappy.

Well, then, if she couldn't run away, what could she do?

"I know what I can do!" Dorothy said right out loud. She was surprised she hadn't thought of it before. She squeezed Raggedy Ann so hard that the doll, if she had a voice, would surely have squealed. "I'll go to Mr. Vancouver's farm and ask him to give me all his newspapers. Then Mama will see I'm not really shy at all. I just don't like piano recitals!"

CHAPTER FOUR

Mama's Birthday

On Sunday morning it seemed as though all out-doors celebrated Mama's birthday. The sky was blue, the grass was green. The birds were noisy and the big old apple tree in the front yard had begun to open its thousands of tight pink buds.

Dorothy and Anabelle were in their secret hiding place under the porch, putting finishing touches on the birthday cards they were making for Mama. Two bright May baskets, woven of strips of colored paper, waited to be filled with flowers. And far back under the porch, where it wouldn't get crushed or accidentally tipped over by the girls, was the fern Daddy had helped them buy.

There was just one trouble: Daddy was sitting on a porch rocker, reading the *Portland Oregonian*.

The girls didn't dare make any noise, or he would hear them. And it usually took Daddy hours to finish reading his Sunday paper. They were trapped.

"How's this?" whispered Anabelle, showing her card to Dorothy. Anabelle had drawn a page full of wavery yellow daffodils and unsteady blue-birds.

"Ssh!" Dorothy pointed up toward the floor of the porch and shook her head violently. Then she went on with her own card, which had a scalloped border outlined in yellow and violet. She was printing "Happy Birthday, Best Mother" in blue, with orange shading to make each letter stand out.

The rocker over their heads creaked. Daddy left the porch and strolled off toward Main Street. That was funny, Daddy going to town on a Sunday morning. But no matter, the important thing was that now the coast was clear.

"Come on," said Dorothy, fitting her orange and blue crayons back into their box, "let's go pick flowers."

The girls crept cautiously out of their head-quarters. They wandered about the house, eyes to the ground, looking for flowers to fill their baskets. There were plenty to choose from. "Hold out your skirt," said Dorothy. She picked clover blossoms and buttercups, dandelions and blue flax and violets, and put them into Anabelle's cupped pinafore.

"How about these?" Anabelle's toe pointed to Mama's tulip and daffodil bed.

Dorothy picked a few of the littlest ones. "I don't think there are any roses yet, but let's go see."

With Anabelle carefully holding her skirt container in front of her knees, the two girls went around to the other side of the yard. Here a line of rose bushes formed one boundary of their property. They saw dozens of buds, every one a tight little knob of green. It was hard to believe that fat roses, with petals of red or yellow, lay wrapped inside these tiny packages.

"Shall we pick some buds?" Anabelle sounded doubtful.

"They're not pretty yet," Dorothy decided. "Anyway, I think we have enough flowers."

The girls crept back into their cave. They heaped the flowers carefully into the two baskets. Anabelle's handle came unstuck and Dorothy helped her paste it back again. As a final touch each girl

hid her birthday card, folded very tiny, among the blooms.

Dorothy checked to make sure nobody was watching. She carried the potted fern to a hiding place behind the trunk of the apple tree. She tip-toed onto the porch, with Anabelle close behind, and placed the May baskets to one side of the door. "Ready?" she whispered.

Anabelle nodded. Two fists rapped sharply on the front door. The girls scampered off the porch and hurried to get out of sight behind the apple tree.

Peeking around its trunk, they saw the door open. Mama stepped out. She looked up and down the street. Dorothy looked too. Not a soul in sight.

Steam from the kitchen had turned Mama's hair into loose, soft curls that no hairpins could hold down. Her eyes were as green as her apron. Dorothy thought she was a very pretty mother.

Mama walked from one end of the porch to the other, and back again. "Who could have knocked?" she asked herself loudly. "I guess I'll have to give up." She started slowly toward the front door.

Suddenly, then, she noticed the baskets. "Gracious, what beautiful baskets! What lovely flowers!"

Mama stooped to scoop up the baskets, being careful not to pull on their frail handles. With a basket in the palm of each hand, she smelled one, and then the other. "What fragrance! I wonder who gave these to me?" she asked the air around her in a very clear voice.

Mama sat down in the wicker rocker and examined the baskets more closely. She found the notes, and unfolded and read them. "How pleasant!" she said distinctly. "Now if I only knew who sent me these wonderful birthday wishes!"

Anabelle could contain herself no longer. She yanked her arm from Dorothy's grasp and rushed up to the porch. Dorothy followed. Mama hugged and kissed her girls and thanked them kindly.

"I suppose you think May baskets are babyish," said Dorothy. "So do I. I just made one to help Anabelle."

"I'm not a baby either!" Anabelle stamped her foot. "I'm eight years old! I made my own basket!"

"You managed beautifully, both of you," said Mama. She put her arm around Dorothy's shoulders. "My birthday wouldn't be the same without the May baskets, Dorothy. I love to keep up old customs. I only hope you'll both want to surprise me every birthday for as long as I live."

"This isn't everything," said Anabelle, jumping up and down with excitement. "There's more. You get it, Dorothy."

Dorothy ran behind the apple tree and picked up the heavy fern. She clasped the red clay pot to her stomach and peered through fern fronds to see where she was going. Dorothy carried the pot onto the porch and set it down at Mama's feet. The fern's branches spouted up and out like a flowing green fountain.

"Oh, you wonderful children," said Mama, kissing each daughter in turn. "What an enormous fern! It'll look beautiful in the bay window where the rubber plant used to be."

"Daddy paid for some of it," explained Anabelle. "We didn't have enough money."

"Are you sure you wouldn't rather have had new stockings?" asked Dorothy. "Not cotton stockings. Real silk ones, for dressing up?"

"I prefer the fern," said Mama firmly. "I wouldn't trade it for stockings, not for all the tea in China."

Dorothy smiled with satisfaction. She knew that was what Mama would say.

Mama looked around. "Where's your daddy? I want to thank him, too."

"He went downtown," said Dorothy. "What for?"

"I don't know. I just hope he gets back before my dinner is overcooked. Dorothy, why don't you practice now, before we eat?"

"Oh, Mama, do I *have* to practice today? On your birthday?"

Mama hesitated a moment. Then she smiled. "All right, we'll let it go. I guess one day away from the piano won't make too much difference." She picked up the plant. "Don't go far from the house, girls. I'll be calling you to dinner soon." Mama and the fern disappeared inside.

"What'll we do now?" Anabelle asked.

"Let's play sick," said Dorothy promptly. She ran to the side yard where the rose bushes were. "Come on, Anabelle, you be nurse."

"I was nurse last time," Anabelle protested.

"I said it first," said Dorothy. She lay comfortably up a slight slope. "I'm sick," she announced. "Take my temperature."

Anabelle broke a branch off a rose bush and carefully removed leaves, buds, and sharp green thorns. She stuck this thermometer into her patient's mouth. While she waited for it to register she felt Dorothy's head with her wrist. "You're feverish," she said. "I'll have to put on a cold compress."

Anabelle picked some of the biggest rose-bush leaves and placed them over Dorothy's forehead. Then she removed the thermometer from Dorothy's mouth and squinted at it gravely. "You're really quite ill. You've got la grippe. I'm afraid you'll have to eat this bad-tasting medicine." Anabelle began to roll some grass into pills.

But Dorothy said, "Not grass! This time the medicine has to be bread and butter."

"What if Mama's in the kitchen?" said Anabelle. Both girls knew that Mama did not allow eating between meals, and most especially not before Sunday dinner. On Sundays the family ate its main meal at midday.

"Wait until she goes out," said Dorothy.

Anabelle left her patient and trotted obediently off toward the back door. Dorothy lay with the sun on her eyelids while her imagination followed Anabelle into the kitchen. She saw Anabelle cutting a slice of Mama's crusty white bread. Dorothy's mouth watered. She hoped it would be a thick slice, and that Anabelle would remember to spread the butter evenly to all the edges.

Anabelle returned to her charge under the rose

bush. She broke the bread into pill-sized bites and began to feed them to the sick patient. Dorothy tried to pretend the pills were bitter and she didn't want them. This was hard to do because the bread really was delicious. Soon the slice was all gone.

"I'm definitely better," Dorothy announced to her nurse. "But I'm not all well yet. I need more pills. This time put apricot jam on top of the butter."

"If I do, will you let me eat some pills too?"

"But you're not sick."

"Let's take turns, then," begged Anabelle. "It's my turn to be sick!"

Before Dorothy could reply she heard a long, shrill whistle. She would recognize that whistle anywhere. She brushed the leaves from her forehead and jumped to her feet. "Daddy's coming! Let's go meet him!"

But Anabelle knew the whistle as well as anybody. She was already streaking off down the street.

To Dorothy's surprise, Daddy was not walking. "Where did you get the bicycle?" she shouted as she ran toward him. "Who is it for?"

CHAPTER FIVE

Another Present for Mama

Daddy got off the bicycle to avoid being tipped over and drowned in a tide of daughters. "Whose is it?" "Will you give me a ride?" "What'll Mama say?" They swarmed around the bicycle admiring its redness, its bigness, the metal basket strapped in front of the handlebars.

Daddy covered his ears in mock distress. "What a hen yard!"

Mama heard the hullabaloo and came running down the porch steps. "What is this, Avram, one of your jokes?"

"A birthday present for you," teased Daddy. He pinched Mama's cheek. "Admit it, haven't you always wanted to ride a bicycle?"

"Give me a ride in the basket, Daddy, will you? Will you?" Anabelle jumped up and down, tugging at her father's arm.

"Calm down, Anabelle." Mama was standing with her hands on her hips, waiting for Daddy's explanation.

"I swapped this with one of my customers for a wheelbarrow," he said. "It's not a new bicycle but it's in good condition and sturdy. Max will use it. I'm counting on Max to help me out in the store after school."

Mama looked relieved. "That's a good idea," she nodded. "I thought for a minute you intended to give it to Dorothy. You know how I feel about girls riding bicycles."

Daddy said, "Jennie, my old-fashioned Jennie, the world has changed since you were a child. This is 1921, whether you like it or not. Girls *do* ride bicycles nowadays. I'll even wager that when Dorothy and Anabelle grow up they'll be driving automobiles, too."

There was a note of impatience in Daddy's voice. Dorothy took Mama's hand and squeezed it to show sympathy. She knew how it felt to be scolded.

"Now can I have a ride?" Anabelle asked, pulling at Daddy's coat to get his attention.

"Well . . ." Daddy fingered the frame. "I just

painted it last night and this bar is still a bit sticky. . . ."

"That settles it," said Mama. "My roast is out of the oven and I don't want it to get cold. To-morrow, Anabelle."

Anabelle, grumbling and protesting, tagged Daddy around back to the tool shed to store the bicycle. Dorothy followed Mama into the kitchen, where the air vibrated with the odors of savory things to eat.

"I cooked everything I like best," Mama confessed, when the family was assembled around the table. "After all, it's my birthday."

This was a holiday occasion, so a white linen tablecloth covered the everyday oilcloth. Mama had arranged the flowers from the May baskets in a sparkling cut-glass bowl. She served roast lamb and crisp potato pancakes, homemade applesauce and tiny green beans. Dorothy decided that when it was her birthday she would ask Mama to cook the same dinner for her. Anabelle might call her a copycat but she didn't care. She liked everything Mama liked, right down to the chocolate cake with walnuts in the frosting.

"How about going for a ride this afternoon?" asked Daddy, stirring his final glass of hot tea.

"We haven't done that for quite a while."

"Can I sit in your lap and hold the reins?" asked Anabelle.

"Will you be sure and ask for Margery?" Dorothy begged.

Whenever the family went anywhere, Daddy hired a horse and buggy from Swenson's Livery Stables. Dorothy's favorite horse was Margery, a placid white creature with the longest eyelashes Dorothy had ever seen.

"We'll see." Daddy got up from the table, grinning broadly.

"Can I come with you?" asked the ever-ready Anabelle.

"No, Anabelle, we said we'd wash the dishes for Mama, remember? It's part of our birthday present, we decided," Dorothy added to Mama.

"I don't want to do any old dishes, I want to go with Daddy."

Dorothy stamped her foot. "Anabelle, you promised!"

"I don't care," said Anabelle hotly. "It was your idea, so you can do it."

"That makes you a liar!"

"If I'm a liar, you're another," retorted Anabelle. "Remember the time you——"

"Stop this silly squabbling," said Daddy. "If you're going to do your Mama a favor, do it cheerfully. You might as well help, Anabelle, because I want to go to town by myself this time."

Daddy put on his hat and left. Dorothy ran hot water over the mountains of greasy dishes heaped in the sink, while Anabelle began to clear the table. Both girls worked slowly at first because they still felt cross. But Mama helped too, singing softly as she shook crumbs from the tablecloth and swept the floor. Soon the work went easily. Mama scrubbed the heavy pots and pans and washed out the sink, while Dorothy helped Anabelle dry the silverware.

When the dishes were all put away and the towels rinsed and spread to dry, Mama looked around at her orderly kitchen. "I never had a nicer birthday, you lovely children," she said, her face pink with pleasure. "You can't imagine how I enjoy seeing you grow into such capable girls."

Mama bent to replace the roasting pan where it belonged under the drainboard. As she straightened up she said, "My birthday happiness would be complete, Dorothy, if we could tell Miss Michaels that you are going to be in the recital. It would give me such special pleasure to know you are able to play the piano for other people's enjoyment."

Dorothy didn't know what to say. Why, oh why, hadn't she gone to get those papers from Mr. Vancouver? Maybe there was still time to do it. The recital must be very important for Mama to ask a favor like this. Mama generally just told the girls what they had to do.

While Dorothy was hesitating, they all heard the urgent noise of a car horn. Uh-*ooga*! it went, uh-*ooga*, uh-*ooga*, uh-*ooga*, over and over again, as though it were stuck.

Anabelle rushed to the front door. "It's Daddy!" she yelled. "This time he's driving a car!"

They all made a dash outside. Daddy was sitting at the wheel of a black touring car. He opened the door and stepped out, his face wreathed in smiles. "This really is your birthday present, Jennie," he said. "A brand-new six-cylinder Moon. Isn't she a beauty?"

Mama stared at the car. "Another of your jokes?"

"No joke," said Daddy. "It's ours, bought and paid for."

"But where's Margery?" asked Dorothy.

"Margery is safely in her stall at Swenson's. The truth is, Dorothy, that Margery's day is coming to an end. From now on this family rides in a horseless carriage. How do you like the new buggy?"

The Moon was long and shiny, with spoked wooden wheels and a canvas roof. The ornament on its radiator cap was a beautiful silver-colored crescent moon.

Dorothy followed Anabelle onto the running board and into the car. They climbed from the back seat to the front seat, and tugged at the big steering wheel. Dorothy was careful not to touch any of the strange-looking knobs and levers which might start the car.

"Let's go for a ride!" Anabelle slid out of the car and began to climb the sharp ridge of the hood.

"Hop in," Daddy said.

Mama stood on the sidewalk, untying her apron and looking very sad. "I suppose we have to keep up with the times." She sighed. "But oh, how I wish we could just go right on living the way we've always been."

"You'll get used to riding in a car," said Daddy. "In a few years you'll wonder how you ever got along without one. Come on, now."

"Not with my apron on. Wait a minute." Mama hurried back into the house.

Daddy and the girls climbed up into the car. Daddy fiddled with the levers. He adjusted the spark and pulled out the choke and twisted a knob. The motor sputtered, caught on, and roared. "You don't have to crank a Moon," Daddy said proudly. "It's not like one of your cheap tin lizzies."

Mama came down the front walk, struggling to push a hatpin through her broad-brimmed straw hat. "Are you sure it's safe, Avram?" she asked, stopping short at the car door. "Did somebody show you how to drive?"

"What's there to learn?" Daddy asked impatiently. "I drove it this far, didn't I? Come on!"

Mama put a foot on the high running board and held on to one of the metal rods supporting the roof. She hoisted herself up and into the front seat next to Daddy. As she slammed the door, Daddy began to race the motor. There was a grinding noise. The car coughed, jerked forward, then stopped abruptly.

"No need to get alarmed," said Daddy, reading Mama's anxious expression. "I forgot to release the hand brake, that's all. Takes a little time to get used to the feel of the thing." He started the motor again. "All right, now, here we go!" The car bumped down the middle of the road.

"Just look at the dust," said Mama. "Better slow down."

"The faster I go the sooner we'll get away from dust," Daddy replied. "Main Street is paved."

He turned into Main Street and drove past the stores in the business district. Seeing someone he knew walking along, he honked vigorously. The man waved and grinned and yelled good-naturedly, "Git a hoss!"

Soon they were beyond the town. The car bowled along into open countryside, traveling faster than Dorothy had ever gone before. It made her dizzy to see trees whizzing by. Mama clutched her handbag but Daddy sat straight and proud, whistling as he drove.

The Moon started down a long hill. It began to pick up speed.

"Shouldn't you slow down?" said Mama nervously. The car picked up more speed. "For my sake?"

Daddy stopped whistling. The car went faster. And faster.

"Avram!" shrieked Mama.

"Be quiet!" roared Daddy. He switched off the motor. "Can't you see I'm doing the best I can?"

Daddy hunched over the steering wheel. The car lurched violently this way and that as he tried to avoid ruts in the road. Dorothy's head thwacked against a metal post.

The Moon came to the bottom of the hill. It jounced over a hump in the road and coasted slowly to a stop. Dorothy rubbed her head where, sure enough, a lump was already rising.

There was a long silence. When Daddy finally spoke, his voice was small and thin. "I got the gas pedal mixed up with the brake," he said. "It could happen to anybody."

Mama was crying. "You can't make me like it," she said. "I'm an old-fashioned person and I don't see anything wrong with old-fashioned ways."

Daddy did not answer. He started the car and turned it around. Mama continued to cry. Why didn't Daddy say something?

But he just sat there, while Mama's breath came in little jerks that tore at Dorothy's heart. It was unbearable. Somebody had to say something to cheer Mama up.

So Dorothy stood up in the back of the car and leaned across the front seat to nuzzle her face in Mama's neck.

"Don't cry, Mama," she whispered. "I'll be in the recital."

CHAPTER SIX

Fifty Pounds of Newspapers

"Where's Daddy?" Dorothy asked as she came into the kitchen for breakfast next morning.

"He left early. There's a lot to do at the store today because he won't be there tomorrow. Here, dear, eat your cereal."

Mama set a bowl of oatmeal on the table. Dorothy sprinkled brown sugar on top. "Did he write my excuse for being absent Friday?"

Mama clapped a hand to her forehead. "God in heaven, where are my brains? I forgot to ask him. Dorothy, this time you'll have to write for me." Mama left the room to fetch paper and ink.

Mama had often explained why she couldn't write in English. First Dorothy had been born, and then Anabelle. Taking care of her family had never left Mama time to go to night school the way Daddy had done.

Dorothy stirred her cereal. Here in the family it didn't matter one bit that Mama couldn't write English. She spoke as well as anybody. Dorothy didn't even think Mama's accent was foreign. But when it came to sending notes to school . . . Dorothy squirmed, and wished Daddy had remembered to write the excuse. She dreaded the moment when Mrs. Merrick would recognize Dorothy's own handwriting, and ask why.

Mama returned to the kitchen carrying two sheets of white paper, a red wooden pen-holder and a square bottle of blue-black ink. "You'll have to write a note to Anabelle's teacher, too, because you'll both be out of school tomorrow."

Mama carefully brushed the oilcloth cover to make sure there were no crumbs. She set the paper on the table and unscrewed the top of the bottle of ink. Then she leaned against the drainboard, biting a thumbnail and closing one eye to help herself think. She dictated:

> Monday, May 2, 1921
>
> Dear Mrs. Merrick:
>
> Please excuse Dorothy's absence. She stayed home with a sore throat.

Dorothy will also be out tomorrow because we have to go to Portland to meet a train. I am sorry she is missing so much school.

Very truly yours,

Dorothy handed the pen to Mama. Mama wiped her hands on her apron and sat down at the table. Leaning far forward over the paper, she slowly drew her name. Even Anabelle could write better than that!

Later, when Miss Cole rang the school bell and the children filed into the corridor, Dorothy walked toward her classroom with the note hidden in her lunch bag. She held to a faint hope that Mrs. Merrick would forget to ask for it.

Mrs. Merrick was standing at the door, greeting her students as they entered. When she saw Dorothy she put out her hand and smiled and said, "We missed you Friday."

Dorothy fished up the excuse. She watched Mrs. Merrick's face as she read it. But there was no expression of surprise or disapproval. Perhaps Mrs. Merrick didn't recognize Dorothy's handwriting after all. "Who's going to be on the train tomorrow?" she asked.

"My grandma and Uncle Max," mumbled Dorothy, looking at her shoes.

"That sounds pleasant. Will they be visiting for long?" Mrs. Merrick bent over so she could catch Dorothy's reply.

"They're going to live with us." Dorothy spoke so low it was almost a whisper. She didn't want the other children to hear. "They don't live any place now because they just escaped out of Russia."

"How wonderful for all of you!" Mrs. Merrick was whispering too. "I wish them every happiness in their new homeland." She turned Dorothy away with a smile and a nod. Dorothy walked down the aisle toward her desk hoping Mrs. Merrick hadn't noticed her red face. Her forehead was still burning. If only she could talk to a teacher without blushing!

"Well, well, if it isn't old Dorthy-Porthy," said Edgar Lemon, who sat in the desk directly behind. "I missed you Friday. Phew, what a relief!"

"Leave her alone, gooney," said Enid Stidd from across the aisle.

Dorothy slid into her desk, giving Enid a tiny smile. Enid smiled back, and her cheeks flashed the deep dimples that Dorothy admired so much.

Enid was certainly the prettiest girl in Woodburn. How Dorothy wished that she, too, had silky black hair cut in a Dutch bob. She shook her stupid brown curls so hard her hair ribbon wobbled.

Mrs. Merrick rapped with a ruler and called the class to order. Everybody stood alongside their desks and saluted the flag. They sang the anthem and sat down to another day's work.

"In connection with our geography lesson," said Mrs. Merrick, "I've been meaning to suggest that we plan a little entertainment for our last day in class. Am I right in supposing that almost everybody in this room has relatives who came to America from some other land?"

Many hands went up. The class soon learned that Ruby and Emerald Visceglia had Italian grandparents and that Kitty McCloskey was Irish. Ozro Marschner's father was born in Germany but his mother came from Milwaukee, Wisconsin. Even those children whose parents and grandparents and great-grandparents were born in America told of ancestors who had come from England or France or Canada or a dozen other countries.

Dorothy had an impulse to speak up in class for once, and add Russia to the list. She saw Mrs. Merrick looking in her direction. But the moment passed and Mrs. Merrick went on, "I thought it would be fun if some of you wore native costumes the last day of school. Everyone who wants to can show us their old country's songs or dances. Maybe some of you have interesting stories about how your people came to America. I have a Swedish costume in my attic if anybody would like to borrow it."

Enid Stidd said she would sing an English folk song. The Visceglia twins offered to perform an Italian peasant dance. Ozro Marschner said he could show the class what German money looked like.

Dorothy kept her eyes on her inkwell.

Edgar Lemon was just asking if he could come to school dressed in a Chinese costume, even though he wasn't Chinese, when the door opened and Miss Cole entered.

"Good morning, children," said the principal.

"Good morning, Miss Cole," the class chanted politely.

Miss Cole waited for Mrs. Merrick to come up to the front of the room. Miss Cole was tall and stringy and stiff. Her hair was drawn so tightly back from her forehead that it seemed to pull her eyebrows up.

"I came in to talk with you about the paper drive," said Miss Cole to Mrs. Merrick in a loud whisper which Dorothy could plainly hear. "I am very much dissatisfied with the performance of this class."

"Oh, those aren't our latest figures," said Mrs. Merrick in a low voice. She glanced at the red and yellow chart on the blackboard. "Our paper-drive reporter was absent Friday and she hasn't had a chance to bring her statistics up to date."

"Never mind," replied Miss Cole crossly. "Even with the new figures your class is lagging shamefully."

"I'm sorry," said Mrs. Merrick. Color rose in her face. "Of course I'm glad to accept whatever papers the children bring in, but I don't feel I can force them."

"Keeping after people is the only way to get things done," scolded Miss Cole. She shifted her attention to the class. The room was very quiet. Whenever Miss Cole was present nobody, not even Edgar Lemon, so much as shuffled his feet.

"Where's your class spirit?" Miss Cole asked the upturned faces. "Do you want the whole school to come out ahead of the fifth grade?

"As you've been told many times, the purpose of the paper drive is to buy ourselves a new piano. Now get to work! The next time I talk to Mrs. Merrick I want to hear that every one of you has brought in at least fifty pounds!"

Miss Cole turned on her low rubber heels and left the room. The fifth grade sat in silence, looking at Mrs. Merrick.

Mrs. Merrick sighed. She took off her glasses

and rubbed her eyes. Dorothy noticed two red marks on either side of her teacher's nose where the glasses pinched on.

"We'll talk about the party another time," Mrs. Merrick said at last. "Now, members of the first arithmetic group, bring your homework and come sit up front. The rest of you may go on coloring your maps of Asia."

Life returned to the class as everybody moved to new positions. The rows of desks were bolted to the floor, so the children had to change places whenever the teacher asked for special groups.

Dorothy took her unfinished map and a selection of crayons and went to sit at Ruby's desk. As she outlined India in green she thought how awful it was for Mrs. Merrick to be scolded right in front of everybody. Dorothy wished with all her heart that she could help Mrs. Merrick. If only she could collect fifty—no, a hundred—no, two hundred pounds of paper.

In Dorothy's imagination, every green stroke of her crayon became a bundle of newspapers. Soon there were stacks and stacks of them. They were piled high in the basement. They overflowed the school corridor. Miss Cole saw them and was flabbergasted. Mrs. Merrick was delighted.

The green crayon flew out of Dorothy's hand and broke in half on the floor.

Dorothy's daydream broke, too. As she stooped to pick up the pieces of crayon, she wondered why she bothered to pretend to herself this way. She knew perfectly well she wasn't going to collect any more papers. She hadn't dared to ask anybody so far, not even Mr. Vancouver.

She was just a disappointment to everybody. Most of all to herself.

CHAPTER SEVEN

Getting Ready for Relatives

All was hustle and bustle on Tuesday morning. Mama had the whole family hurrying about making beds, dusting furniture, scraping ashes out of the stove, running into the rain to pick flowers. It was impossible not to feel excited.

"I wish it wasn't raining." Mama paused to look out of the parlor window where she was watering her birthday fern. "I wanted to greet my mother in sunshine."

"Sunshine inside is where it's important," said Daddy, who was almost always in high spirits. "Come on, sweetheart, let's dance the *gazotzka*." He put his hands on his hips and kicked with his toes.

Mama couldn't help smiling. She gave Daddy a little push as she said, "Don't be foolish, Avram.

Our *gazotzka* days are over."

"What's *gazotzka*?" Anabelle asked.

"A wonderful happy Russian dance," said Daddy. "I used to be the best *gazotzka* dancer in the village and I'll bet I still am. Here, children, I'll show you."

Daddy began to hunt through a pile of dusty phonograph records. "Dorothy, will you start the machine?"

Dorothy ran to the Victrola which stood on a small table near the piano. She cranked a handle on its side until the spring that moved the turntable was wound tight. She released a switch and the flat wheel began to turn.

By this time Daddy had found the record he was looking for. He slipped it on the machine and carefully set the needle arm down on the edge. There were a few seconds of scratchy noises. Then out of the lily-shaped horn that was the Victrola's loudspeaker came the muffled, thumping beat of a two-step.

"Now watch a genuine *gazotzka*!" Daddy placed his hands on his hips and bent his knees until he was almost crouching on the floor. He bounced on his right foot while he threw his left leg out to the side. Then he bounced on his left foot and threw his right leg out to the side.

For several kicks Daddy flung his legs crisply. Then he began to pant and fall behind the beat of the music.

"That's enough, Avram," said Mama. "Remember you have to be able to drive to Portland this afternoon."

"It's easy! It's easy! See, I can do the *gazotzka*!" said Anabelle, bouncing up and down.

"So can I!" Dorothy, hands on hips, imitated her father. It was surprisingly hard to crouch and balance and kick all at the same time. In fact, with the second kick she found herself sitting on the carpet.

The record wheezed to an end. Daddy limped over to turn off the phonograph. "Your mother's right, girls," he said. "It's a young man's dance."

"Can Uncle Max do the *gazotzka*?" Anabelle said. "I'm going to ask him."

Mama took charge again. "Dorothy, you'd better practice now. Avram, will you set up the new cot for Anabelle? Anabelle, come help me move your toys."

Dorothy obediently sat down at the piano and began her scales. All the while her mind was fixed on the interesting thumpings and bangings that were going on upstairs.

After a very long time she yelled upstairs to Mama, "Is it time to quit now?"

"It's hardly been twenty minutes," Mama called back. "Better practice the 'Butterfly Waltz' some more."

Dorothy groped her way through the "Butterfly Waltz" and one more scale. When she finished she decided not to bother Mama by asking the time again. Instead, she slid off the piano stool and hurried upstairs to see what was happening.

Anabelle's room was transformed. The freshly ironed curtains were so white they looked almost blue. A bowl of flowers stood on the bureau and the closet had nothing in it but hangers.

Dorothy ran to her own room. It, too, was almost unrecognizable. Her bed was crowded to one side to make room for Anabelle's temporary cot. Anabelle's clothes were squeezed into open drawers and her dresses pushed against Dorothy's in the closet. The floor of the closet was covered with cartons of Anabelle's toys.

"Where's Raggedy Ann?" asked Dorothy, sensing the absence of her doll's familiar shape.

"I put her off into the closet," said Mama, who was busily making up Anabelle's bed.

Dorothy ran to the closet and burrowed about to find her doll.

"Yah! Yah!" Anabelle jeered, pointing a finger. "Dorothy's a baby!"

"Don't tease," said Mama. And then, to Dorothy, "I put her away because there are too many things cluttering this room."

"Raggedy Ann is not a thing!" Dorothy smoothed her doll's dress and combed her fingers tenderly through the red yarn hair.

"All right, Dorothy, don't scold me," said Mama. "I didn't know you still cared about Raggedy Ann. I thought she was just an old habit." Mama straightened the white spread over Anabelle's bed. "Come downstairs, Anabelle. I'll brush your hair now." Mama took Anabelle's hand and hurried out.

Dorothy sat on her bed with Raggedy Ann in her lap. For the last several days she and Anabelle had been looking forward to sharing a bedroom. They thought it would be fun to giggle after the lights were out. They had decided to see if they could lie awake and tell stories all night, and not fall asleep at all.

But now Dorothy felt cross because her room was so very crowded. Her toys were all pushed around and there was hardly space to walk. For the first time it occurred to her that she couldn't play with Raggedy Ann whenever she wanted. Anabelle would see and surely tease her. And if she wasn't alone, how could she practice her dimple-making?

Thinking about dimples reminded Dorothy to

stick her fingers into her cheeks now when she had the chance. She was still convinced that, with patience, she would someday have dimples exactly like Enid Stidd's.

Dorothy put Raggedy Ann aside and settled back against the head of her bed. She pushed her cheeks so hard they hurt. It would be wonderful if Uncle Max, seeing her for the first time this afternoon, turned to Mama and said, "Why, you never wrote me that Dorothy has dimples!"

CHAPTER EIGHT

Meeting Uncle Max

It was time to leave for Portland. Dorothy, still without dimples, climbed gingerly into the back seat of the Moon. She had not been in the car since Sunday's ride, and she didn't relish any more bumps on the head.

Mama was also uneasy. "Are you *sure* you understand all about driving now?" she asked Daddy, who was standing by to hoist her in. "Will you remember where the brake pedal is?"

Daddy gave her a push up and shut the car door. "I guarantee a safe ride. Please relax and leave the driving to me."

True to his word, Daddy drove through the rain as carefully as a kitten walking on glass. But Dorothy scarcely noticed. Her feelings were riding up and down on a teeter-totter of happy excitement and uneasy dread.

First she thought, At last I'm really going to see Grandma and Uncle Max! What does Uncle Max look like? What shall I say when I see him? What will he think of me?

She was sure, in this mood, that Uncle Max was going to be tall and dark and strikingly handsome. He would soon become her best friend. Enid Stidd would want to be her friend, too, just in order to know Uncle Max. He would keep dogs from ever jumping on her. He'd teach her to ride a bicycle, and give her goose bumps with stories about escaping from Russia.

Then the see-saw of her feelings tipped the other way. Suddenly she knew that Uncle Max was going to be just another big boy to be afraid of. He would tease her, like Edgar Lemon, and make life miserable. He would get himself a dog, even though Mama didn't like dogs because they made the house dirty.

Dorothy was deep inside these gloomy thoughts when they reached Portland. She looked at the people with umbrellas hurrying along the paved sidewalks and thought, with fright, how easy it would be to get lost in Portland.

Daddy was just driving across a bridge when a

rain cloud moved over to let some sunshine out. Now the wet pavement sparkled, and so did the Willamette River far below. Portland turned into an exciting place to be. There were hundreds of store windows to look into and tall buildings to stare up at and signs to read. Also, Dorothy remembered that Daddy almost always let the girls buy candy when they came to Portland.

Daddy parked the Moon and led his family into Union Station. Dorothy thought no palace could be larger than this high-ceilinged, concrete, pillared cavern. Hundreds of electric lights were shining, even though it was broad daylight outside. Porters wearing red caps wheeled hand trucks in all directions. Strange people milled about. They stood before the rows of ticket windows or dragged their luggage across the marbled floor or slumped on shiny reddish benches. There was a hum of noise, and above the general hubbub a dozen babies bawled at the top of their lungs.

Dorothy couldn't help it, she reached for Mama's hand. Anabelle, she noticed, was already holding on to Daddy.

Daddy threaded his way across the floor to where a man in a striped shirt and a green celluloid eyeshade was chalking train times on an enormous blackboard.

"The 4:07 from Chicago?" Daddy asked.

The man jerked his thumb toward the black-board. It carried the title, "Arrivals." About half way down a chalked list of numbers Dorothy found #382 from Chicago, due in at 4:07. In a column headed "Estimated Arrival" the man had written "On Time."

Daddy pulled his gold watch out of his vest pocket. He snapped open the lid and read the time. Then he checked his watch with an enormous clock that hung on the wall of the station.

"We're twenty-six minutes early," he said. "Might as well sit down."

"Oh, Avram, my knees are shaking," said Mama, taking his arm. Dorothy noticed little drops of moisture on Mama's forehead and her upper lip.

They sat down on a slippery red bench. Ana-belle's feet dangled, and even Dorothy's patent-leather slippers hardly touched the floor. She chewed the elastic that was supposed to be under her chin keeping her beaver hat on, and fell into her reveries: What *did* Uncle Max look like? It would be nice to have him for a friend, even if he was her uncle. Did anybody else in Woodburn have an uncle who was fourteen years old? Dorothy had always thought an uncle had to be an all-the-way-grown-up man.

Anabelle got restless and began to slide up and down the bench. She accidentally bumped into a lady who was knitting, and the lady gave Anabelle a black look. Mama asked Anabelle to sit still. She made Dorothy stop chewing the elastic. Dorothy took her hat off and gave it to Daddy to hold.

"Why don't you children go over there and buy yourselves some candy?" Daddy pointed across the station. "It'll give you something to do."

Dorothy looked in the direction of Daddy's finger. It seemed very far away from where her parents were sitting.

"We'll be right here watching you the whole time." Daddy fished into a trouser pocket and brought up two nickels. He gave one to Anabelle and the other to Dorothy.

Holding the money tightly in their fists, the girls crossed the station to a stall which sold newspapers, magazines, cigars, cigarettes and candy. They stopped in front of a sloping rack which held the five-cent candy bars. Dorothy read the names on the wrappers: Tootsie Roll. Hawaiian

Fruit Drops. Mr. Goodbar. Necco Wafers. Hoeffler's Centennial Chocolates. Handy Andy's Peanut Candy.

Then she turned to the tall jars of penny candies ranged along the counter. Through the clear glass containers an alluring variety begged to be noticed: striped peppermint sticks, yellow candy corn, red and white jawbreakers, black licorice whips. Gumdrops, butterballs, jelly beans and chocolate kisses—those wonderful mound-shaped chocolate kisses with creamy white insides.

"What are you going to buy?" whispered Anabelle.

"Penny candies, you get more that way," Dorothy whispered back.

But which? Somehow the candies Dorothy liked best were always the ones you got least of. Each time she was a customer she wrestled with the same problem. Should she settle for something like jelly beans in order to get a whole batch of them, because jelly beans were five for a penny? Or jawbreakers, which cost one cent apiece but could be sucked on for hours? Or should she recklessly spend her money on five single, sweet, fast-melting, hauntingly delicious chocolate kisses?

Through the din of the station Dorothy heard

Daddy's familiar high whistle. She turned and saw him standing by the bench, motioning "come" with his arm.

Dorothy gave her sister a nudge. "We have to hurry. I'm going to buy chocolate kisses."

"Me too," said Anabelle.

The candy lady counted out five kisses and put them into a tiny white sack for Anabelle. She did the same for Dorothy. Dorothy popped one candy into her mouth and stored the bag safely in her coat pocket. She and Anabelle ran back across the station to their parents.

"Time to go out to the platform," said Daddy.

They walked to a covered shed full of people and train tracks, past a tremendous black engine. Its wheels alone were as tall as Dorothy. A man in blue overalls was leaning out a side window. He caught Dorothy's staring eyes and waved. Above his head, dark smoke spiraled out of the engine's chimney. Next to the engine was its coal car, piled high with the acrid-smelling black lumps.

Daddy and Mama were walking rapidly now. Dorothy had to trot to keep up. Two men in leather jackets were handing blocks of ice up into a passenger car. Their jackets were stained black with drips from melting ice.

"What's the ice for?" Dorothy asked, tugging at Daddy's coat.

But Daddy pointed up the track. "There she comes!"

A huge round headlight was bearing down on them. Behind this evil eye snaked a long line of passenger cars. The snorting, champing engine seemed headed straight for Dorothy, to run her down and mash her like a mosquito. She seized Mama's hand and made herself as small as she could. The train clacked past in a whirlwind of steam and cinders. It rolled to a stop with a final blast of steam that made Dorothy squeeze her eyes shut and burrow her head against Mama's side.

Mama pulled away her hand and began to run along the platform. Dorothy followed as well as she could, jostled and bumped by hurrying waves of people. For a few moments she lost sight of Mama. The next thing she knew, Mama was hugging and kissing a tiny little lady in a long black coat.

When Dorothy caught up to them, Mama was crying and so was Grandma. Grandma turned to Dorothy, grabbed her and held her close. Grandma smelled musty and stale and Dorothy was glad when she was able to pull herself free.

"This is your Uncle Max," said Daddy.

Dorothy dared one quick upward glance. She saw a stringy boy, much shorter than Daddy, with a cinder smudge on his cheek. He had bushy black hair which needed cutting. He was surrounded by carpetbags and knobby parcels.

"Hello," she mumbled, looking away.

Uncle Max took her hand. "'Ello," he said in English. "You are Anabelle, yes?"

Dorothy was insulted. How could anybody possibly mistake her for an eight-year-old? "That's Anabelle," she said, pointing. "I'm Dorothy."

"Ah, yes," he said, looking vaguely around for Anabelle. "Pleased to make the acquaintance." His accent was terrible. Dorothy hardly understood him.

"Can you dance the *gazotzka*?" Anabelle shrilled over the racket around them.

Apparently Uncle Max did not hear, for now he was offering his hand to Mama. But Mama didn't accept the hand. She threw her arms around his neck and wept. "My brother, my darling little Max!"

Dorothy looked about uneasily. Sure enough, a number of people had stopped to stare with open curiosity. If only Mama would talk more

softly, and not hug people right out in public!

Walking back through the station, the four grown-ups jabbered together in noisy Russian as though they were alone in the world. Dorothy and Anabelle tagged silently behind, Dorothy lugging a parcel Daddy had asked her to carry. It was an awkward shape to hold and there were greasy spots on its rumpled brown-paper wrapping. Dorothy wished Uncle Max would carry his own packages.

By the time they reached the car, the girls still trailing behind, Dorothy was sure she didn't like having relatives around. For one thing, she had never imagined they would look like *this*, so shabby and foreign. And how could she even try to make friends with Uncle Max when he didn't pay the slightest attention to her?

For the ride home Dorothy was placed in the front seat between Daddy and Uncle Max, wedged so tight she couldn't even wriggle. It was boring to sit still for such a long time, not able to understand a word of what Daddy and Uncle Max were saying back and forth across the top of her head. She studied Uncle Max's bony wrists, sticking out from the sleeves of a frayed gray coat. His hands were dirty and there was black under his fingernails. What would Mama say to that?

Suddenly Dorothy remembered one bright spot —her candy. She tried to reach into her pocket but it was mashed tight against Uncle Max.

Her chocolate kisses were all melted and ruined!

CHAPTER NINE

Uncle Max Goes to School

In the morning Mama and Daddy talked in whispers. When Dorothy tried to tell Anabelle something at the breakfast table, Mama shushed her. Mama pointed to the swinging door between the kitchen and the parlor. The door, which was always kept open, was closed now because Uncle Max was asleep on the leather sofa in the parlor. With that door shut the whole kitchen looked different.

"Good-by, Jennie. Be good, girls," said Daddy softly, making ready to leave for his store. As he kissed Dorothy he said, "I'm going to take Max over to school this afternoon. I'll tell him to wait for you in the yard when the bell rings, so you can walk home together."

Dorothy was astonished. She forgot to whisper.

"Is Uncle Max going to school?"

At the same moment Anabelle squealed, "He's grown up!"

"Ssh, girls, keep your voices down," cautioned Daddy. "No, Anabelle, Max isn't a man yet. He needs to go to school."

"But he's too big for our school," said Dorothy.

"Yes, I know," whispered Daddy. "I expect he'll only be in the eighth grade for a few weeks, to learn more English. Later we'll see about sending him off to high school. Be nice to him, Dorothy, he feels strange."

Dorothy felt strange, too, at the idea of having an uncle in her school. She hoped none of her classmates would find out. She wished she didn't have to walk home with Uncle Max. If she lingered in her room after the bell rang, maybe he'd get tired of waiting and leave with Anabelle.

At two o'clock that afternoon Mrs. Merrick decided to review homonyms with her fifth grade. She was writing "dough" and "doe" on the board when the door opened and Miss Cole marched in. Behind Miss Cole was Uncle Max.

Dorothy's throat filled up. She put down her pencil and strained to hear what Miss Cole was saying to Mrs. Merrick. The whole class stared at Uncle Max. He stood motionless, looking at nothing. His face was red and there was a foolish half-smile on his lips. He wore one of Daddy's jackets and the sleeves were so long they came down to his fingertips. Mama must have tried to give him a haircut and the result was horribly uneven.

Miss Cole rapped on Mrs. Merrick's desk with

a ruler. "Children, here is an immigrant lad who wishes to become more proficient in English. Since he is related to one of your classmates, I thought it appropriate to place him in this room. I know you will treat him with every kindness. His name is Max." Miss Cole nodded to Mrs. Merrick and left the room.

Everybody except Dorothy craned and twisted and asked one another eager questions. "Max who?" "Which classmate?" Edgar Lemon pulled on one of Dorothy's curls. He leaned forward and whispered, "Hey, do you know Max?"

"Let's get on with our spelling lesson," said Mrs. Merrick. She picked up the chair behind her desk and walked with it toward the back of the room. "Edgar, tell us what a homonym is." Mrs. Merrick invited Uncle Max to sit on her chair at the back of the room. Although Uncle Max was not as big as Daddy, he was far too large for the desks in the fifth grade classroom. "Well, Edgar?"

Edgar stood beside his desk and shuffled his boots. "A honomyn is——"

"Not honomyn. Homonym. *Homonym*."

"Yeah, honomyn. Uh—uh—I forget, Mrs. Merrick."

"Sit down, Edgar. Emerald, do you know?"

Emerald stood up, giggling. The moment Edgar was in his desk again he yanked Dorothy's curl and said, "Do you?"

Dorothy gave the tiniest nod possible. "Your brother?" Edgar persisted.

Dorothy ignored Edgar. She tried to listen to Emerald's recitation, but she heard it from a great distance because of the roaring in her ears. Her throat hurt and she wanted to go home.

From far away, Ozro Marschner finally explained that homonyms were words which sounded alike but were spelled differently and had different meanings. Various children went to the blackboard and wrote sets of homonyms: through and threw; bare and bear; two and too and to.

Dorothy understood now what Mama meant when she said she had eyes in the back of her head. Without ever once looking around at Uncle Max, Dorothy knew that he was sitting stiffly in Mrs. Merrick's chair. Her classmates were swiveling around to sneak glances at the awkward stranger. They whispered and tittered and somehow everybody knew he was Dorothy's uncle.

Dorothy prayed for the closing bell. Edgar Lemon leaned low across his desk and recited to Dorothy's back:

"Dorothy had a little man
   His hair was black as soot
   And everywhere that Dorothy went
   Her uncle followed suit."

Out in the corridor Miss Cole rang the bell at last. There was a mighty thumping of lids as the fifth grade pupils dumped books inside desks. The children lined up in front of the door, first the girls and then the boys. Mrs. Merrick stood at the head of the line, saying good night to her pupils.

Dorothy lingered, pretending to have trouble stacking her books. She did not look at Uncle Max and he did not look at her. He brushed past Mrs. Merrick's pleasant, "Good night, Max" and almost ran out of the room.

Mrs. Merrick began to straighten up her own desk. Dorothy hoped to glide out unnoticed, but her teacher looked up and said, "Dorothy, will you tell your parents I'm going to drop by this evening? I want to have a little chat with them."

Dorothy nodded, unable to speak. Mrs. Merrick had never met Mama and Daddy. No teacher had ever come to their house. What could she possibly want?

Outside, the schoolyard was almost deserted.

Neither Uncle Max nor Anabelle was in sight. Dorothy walked slowly home, worrying about Mrs. Merrick. Was she going to complain about Dorothy's poor showing in the paper drive? Or was she cross because of having Uncle Max in her class?

"Isn't Max with you?" asked Mama the minute Dorothy came in the back door. Anabelle was already sitting at the table nibbling cookies. Grandma, holding a pitcher of milk, came over to Dorothy to kiss her cheek. Grandma's hair was freshly washed and this time she smelled of soap and lavender.

"*Y'di, golubka, y'di,*" said Grandma, patting the table. She poured a glass of milk for Anabelle and another for Dorothy. Then she sat down, nodding with pleasure as Dorothy sank her teeth into a plump spice cookie.

"I waited for Uncle Max." Anabelle was indignant. "But he pushed right past me. I called and called and he wouldn't even listen."

Mama helped herself to a cookie. "Well, we won't worry about Max," she decided. "A boy who came all the way from Russia isn't going to get lost in Woodburn. Do your practicing now, Dorothy, and then you can go out to play."

CHAPTER TEN

Mrs. Merrick's Visit

Twilight was gathering by the time Uncle Max came home. He frowned at Grandma's questions and answered her in short, sharp-sounding phrases. Dorothy did not need to know Russian to understand that Uncle Max wanted to be left alone.

At the supper table Uncle Max sat sullen and silent, but Daddy noticed nothing amiss. "Let's talk English as much as possible," he said, cheerful as usual. He was cutting thick slices of bread from the loaf that stood on a wooden board in front of him. "It's the quickest way to learn. Well, Max, how did you get on in school today?"

Max put down his soup spoon. He struggled for words to express himself. He made a contemptuous spitting noise. "I go back never. *Nikogda.*"

Daddy stopped the bread knife in mid-slice. "What happened?"

"School is for babies," said Uncle Max. "I need it not. I find a job, I work."

Daddy finished cutting the slice. "You're mistaken, Max." He spoke very earnestly. "In this country education is everything. I want to see you through high school, maybe even college. Your whole life depends on the road you take now."

Uncle Max's face showed that he was not following everything Daddy said. Daddy repeated it in Russian.

But Max shook his head and said, "*Nyet*. I go to work."

"I don't understand," said Daddy. "Last night you were eager about going to school. You were so excited when I left you in Miss Cole's office this afternoon. Why have you——"

Daddy was interrupted by somebody rapping at the front door. Everybody except Dorothy looked surprised. "Who could it be at this hour?" asked Mama, hastily untying her apron.

"I forgot to tell you," Dorothy said in a small voice. "It's Mrs. Merrick."

"Why Mrs. Merrick?" Mama was alarmed. Like Dorothy, she thought a visit from a teacher must mean bad news.

Daddy and Mama hastened to the front door. Dorothy wished she dared run and hide in her room. She looked around the familiar kitchen with the unfriendly eyes of a stranger. There hung Grandma's wash, on a rack near the stove. Didn't other families always hang their clothes out on the line? There sat Daddy's glass of tea, while Dorothy knew that real Americans used cups and saucers. There sat Grandma herself, unable to speak English. And Uncle Max, who was much too big to be in Mrs. Merrick's room.

Dorothy got up to run away just as Mrs. Merrick came in. "It was thoughtless of me to get here so early," she was saying to Mama. "Really, I wouldn't mind waiting in the parlor."

"No, please. Sit, sit." Daddy drew up a chair while Mama hastily brushed bread crumbs from the table.

Mrs. Merrick nodded pleasantly to everyone in the room. Dorothy sat down again, hoping her blush would pass unnoticed.

"May I give you a bite to eat?" Mama hurried to the cupboard to fetch a plate. Dorothy sat with her eyes on her own plate, which had a big chip out of one edge. She prayed Mama would not make any mistake in her grammar.

"Thank you, I had my supper an hour ago. I eat alone so I don't spend much time on it."

Mama's face was full of sympathy. "You're a widow, then?"

"Mr. Merrick died three years ago. That's when I went back to teaching."

Dorothy thought it wasn't right for Mama to ask a teacher personal questions. But Mama went on, "No children?"

So far Mrs. Merrick didn't seem angry. She smiled and said, "Plenty of children." She looked at Dorothy. "Twenty-three this year. I spend all day with them, and at night I lie awake wondering how I can do a better job of teaching."

"At least you'll take a cup of tea?"

"Yes, if I may try it in a glass. Yours looks so beautiful in that tall glass. I'm sure it tastes delicious that way, too."

Mama fetched a clean tumbler and filled it with steaming amber tea. She served Mrs. Merrick the tea and offered her a plate of spice cookies.

"I've come to see you about Max," said Mrs. Merrick, stirring her tea and accepting a cookie.

Uncle Max, who had been silently eating his supper, put down his fork at the mention of his name. His eyes followed every expression of Mrs. Merrick's face as she went on. "Miss Cole and I have some difference of opinion about Max's grade placement. I don't believe he belongs in the fifth grade with Dorothy."

"In the *fifth* grade?" said Mama.

"Didn't either of the children tell you? He was in my room this afternoon."

"I expected him to be in the eighth grade," said Daddy. "I thought he could go to the county high school in the fall. There are only a few weeks of school left this year and I hated to send him clear off to Hubbard while he still feels so strange."

"You're quite right," said Mrs. Merrick. "I think Max would have a hard time in high school right now. I've come to ask whether you'll let me teach him privately for the time being."

"What does she say?" Uncle Max asked Daddy.

Daddy and Max exchanged rapid Russian. Daddy reported, "He says he realized this afternoon that he's not a child any more. He wants to go to work."

"Please tell Max that grown-ups can learn as well as children. Please tell him I thought we'd study together in the evenings, so there's no reason he can't work, too. Except, of course, it might be hard to find a job until his English is more fluent. Tell him our studies will help him with his work."

"What is she speaking?" Uncle Max turned to Daddy.

Max listened earnestly as Daddy explained.

"My house is rather far from here," said Mrs. Merrick, helping herself to another cooky. "It's that small brown place on the old Mill River road."

"Max has a bicycle, he can ride over in no time. You must be renting from old Mr. Vancouver?"

"Yes, he's my neighbor." Mrs. Merrick rose to go. "Those are the most delicious cookies," she said to Mama. "Would you give me the recipe?"

Mama smiled. "My mother baked them this afternoon, but she claims they aren't right because she doesn't know my oven yet. Wait, I'll ask how she makes them."

Mama and Grandma spoke. Grandma smiled and nodded to Mrs. Merrick while Mama said, "She has no recipe, she just uses a pinch of this and a cup of that. But if you want to stop in some day after school she'll be glad to make more and show you."

"I would love to come," said Mrs. Merrick, shaking hands with Grandma. "I'll choose a rainy afternoon because these cookies remind me of my mother. She liked to bake when it rained. The warm kitchen helped her rheumatism and the warm cookies consoled me for not being able to play outdoors."

Mama laughed. "I do the same thing. I guess people are alike the world over."

Mrs. Merrick said, "Am I going to see you tomorrow evening, Max?"

"Perhaps yes. At what time, please?"

"The earlier the better. We have a lot of ground

to cover." Mrs. Merrick smiled at the girls, shook hands again with Grandma, and followed Mama and Daddy down the hall toward the front door.

"This is a very kind lady," said Max, speaking directly to Dorothy for the first time.

Dorothy felt warm all over. "I like her the best of any teacher I ever had."

"What could I give her a——" Max's hands fluttered for a word.

"You mean like a present? A gift?" Dorothy picked up the sugar bowl and offered it to Uncle Max.

"No, no." He brushed the sugar bowl aside. "I want to *do* her something big."

"A favor?"

"Yes, a favor. What can I do her a favor?"

Dorothy thought of the jobs Mama found hardest. "You can keep Mrs. Merrick's woodbox full, and clean ashes out of her stove and carry them to the garden." Dorothy ran over to the stove to point out the objects she mentioned. She acted out swinging an axe to chop kindling and using a shovel to clean ashes from the grate.

Uncle Max nodded. "This I do for her gladly. But what can I do her a favor? *Osobyenny.* Mmm, how do you say?" Uncle Max snapped his fingers.

He leaned toward Dorothy, his face concentrated in the search for the right word. His eyes, Dorothy noticed, were the same shade of milk-chocolate brown as her favorite candy kisses.

"You mean 'special'?" she suggested.

Uncle Max bobbed his head energetically up and down. "*Da, da*. Special."

Dorothy began to pace back and forth across the kitchen to help herself think. A splendid idea came to her, the very thing to please Mrs. Merrick. "The paper drive!"

"What means paper drive?"

"I'll tell you!" Dorothy was excited. "Mrs. Merrick needs to have lots of newspapers so Miss Cole can buy a piano for the school. If you'll come with me, I can ask everybody in Woodburn for their papers. We'll collect more paper than old Miss Cole ever saw!"

CHAPTER ELEVEN

Asking for Newspapers

A week passed. Uncle Max was working now in Daddy's hardware store, and every evening he studied with Mrs. Merrick. Dorothy waited patiently for him to find time to go ring doorbells with her.

"The paper drive is almost ended," she finally dared to say one evening as Uncle Max was again getting ready to leave for Mrs. Merrick's.

"Wait for me after school tomorrow then." Uncle Max tightened the leather strap that held his books together. "I ask your daddy's permission to go early home."

The next afternoon Dorothy practiced her music, as usual, and then waited in the front yard for Uncle Max. She and Anabelle crouched over the walk, trying to see what new animals they could make up out of its cracks. Dorothy had just found a monkey when Uncle Max pedaled up. "Come on," he said, resting one foot on a porch step to keep his bicycle upright.

"Where are you going? Can I come too?" Anabelle asked.

"Makes no difference to me. Can she come, Dorothy?"

Dorothy hesitated. She was looking forward to having Uncle Max all to herself for once, so they could really make friends. If Anabelle came along she'd do all the talking, as usual, and that would spoil everything.

"Not now, Anabelle," Dorothy said.

The corners of Anabelle's mouth turned down in an ominous way. "Don't cry, little one," said Uncle Max. "Shall you have a ride around the block before we go?"

Anabelle immediately scrambled up on the bicycle in front of Uncle Max. She held tight to the handlebars and screamed with delight as he swooped off around the corner.

"More! More!" she shrieked as they arrived again in front of the house.

Uncle Max stopped his bicycle and gently put Anabelle off. "Is no time for more. Dorothy, you wish to ride?"

Although Mama always said that bicycles were not for girls, Dorothy had long yearned to ride one anyhow. Now at last her chance had come!

She rapidly scanned the parlor windows to make sure Mama was not watching. No Mama shape was visible behind the lace curtains. Her heart beating fast with excitement, Dorothy hoisted herself onto the bicycle bar. Off they went, leaving a sorrowing Anabelle behind.

"Tell me where we go." Uncle Max pedaled hard to carry his weight and Dorothy's up the road. Dorothy's legs were stuck stiffly to one side, out of the way of Uncle Max's circling knee.

In truth, Dorothy didn't know quite where to begin. It was no use asking for newspapers at any house in the immediate neighborhood. She had already seen children knocking on all those doors.

She considered various places as they wheeled past. Not this gabled house, because Ruby and Emerald Visceglia lived here. Not that white building; it was the Methodist Church. A church didn't have newspapers to give away. The little brown shingled house next to the church was where the Methodist minister lived. Dorothy knew him by sight but wouldn't dare ask him for papers, not even with Uncle Max along.

They came to the end of the road and turned into Main Street. They went by half a dozen cars parked along the wooden sidewalks and several horses hitched to the curbs. Dorothy peeked into Daddy's hardware store as they passed. He was talking to a customer and didn't see her.

On they went. Past Fairley's Drug Store, the post office, the butcher shop. "Any of these?" asked Uncle Max.

Dorothy shook her head. Stores were the first place children went when they were asking for papers.

They rode past Swenson's Livery Stables with its pungent horsy smell. Past the Woodburn Notion & Variety Shop, whose show window was full of speckled crêpe paper and fading Easter baskets. Now came another row of houses.

Dorothy's bottom was beginning to feel dented where the iron bar of the bicycle cut in. Then she saw Enid Stidd just ahead, sitting alone on her front stoop. All discomfort vanished and Dorothy sat up as straight as she could. There was nobody in the world she would rather have see her riding on a bicycle.

And Enid did see her. Enid stood up and waved.

She called, "Hey, will you ask your uncle to give me a ride, too?"

Dorothy smiled and waved back. "Some other time," she yelled, and Enid was left enviously behind.

Uncle Max turned into a little thread of a back road that joined the main street shortly beyond Enid's house.

Being seen by Enid made Dorothy giddy with courage. "We'll ask here," she announced. She pointed out a small house almost hidden behind its overgrown shrubbery. It was a house she had never noticed before.

Uncle Max braked to a stop, and Dorothy stood and stretched her stiffened legs. Uncle Max leaned the bicycle against a chestnut tree. "Remember, you talk, I listen," he said. "My English is still for shame."

A dog barked inside the house and immediately Dorothy had doubts. She hesitated until Uncle Max made an impatient gesture. "Come on!"

The dog was still barking, and all of a sudden the project of asking a stranger for newspapers was too rich for Dorothy's blood. She backed up against the tree trunk. "I'd rather wait here. You ask."

"But you promised me! Is your idea!"

Dorothy couldn't answer. She just looked at Uncle Max. He stared back at her with an expression in which Dorothy saw impatience and scorn. Finally he twitched his shoulders, turned away and marched up to the door. He twisted the old-fashioned doorbell and Dorothy heard its long, shrill ring inside.

The dog raised his barks to a level announcing the end of the world. Dorothy was glad she had decided to stay back. She peered up from behind her shadowed haven. The door opened and there stood Miss Cole!

"Well, young man," Miss Cole said in her cold voice. "What is it?"

Uncle Max was so surprised he had trouble talking. "I—well—you see—the paper drive—"

"Since you are not a pupil at Woodburn School, I cannot see what concerns you about the paper drive," said Miss Cole. Each word was wrapped in icicles. "If this is some kind of a joke, Max, I am not amused." She nodded curtly and shut the door.

Max stared at the door a moment. Then he ran down from the porch. His face was on fire, his brown eyes sparkled with fury.

"So you enjoy jokes?" he shouted at Dorothy.

"You find funny to make me foolish?"

"Oh, no!" Dorothy cried out. "I didn't know it was Miss Cole's house! Cross my heart and hope to die!"

But Uncle Max was too angry to hear. "Well, I have enough words for you!" he roared. "You're a big baby!" He mounted his bicycle. "Also a coward!" He rode away, turning to call back over his shoulder, "From now you leave me alone!"

Dorothy was stunned. Holding back tears, she ran after Uncle Max. But as she ran his words sounded over and over in her head. A coward and a baby. He hated her. He would hate her forever and it was her own fault. She never did anything right. She was a baby and a coward.

When Dorothy got back to the main road she did not turn left, in the direction of home. She ran north along the highway, toward the open country and Portland. She was running senselessly, but when she came to the old Mill River turnoff she swung into it.

By this time she could hardly draw a breath. A sharp pain was sticking her side. She collapsed by the road to rest, her chest heaving, her face steaming. She didn't want to go home. How could she ever face Uncle Max again?

This was the road Mr. Vancouver lived on. Dorothy thought about Mr. Vancouver, with his soft, drawling voice. If she marched to his farm, right this minute, he would give her papers. She knew he would. Then she could hand over the bundle to Uncle Max and prove that at least she was not a coward.

Dorothy hesitated. She knew Mr. Vancouver liked her and would be nice to her, yet she was afraid of going alone to his door. Of course there was Nipper to worry about, but it was more than that. It was that old shyness, that black, unreasonable, shrinking dread of being noticed.

Dorothy picked a roadside dandelion and twisted it blindly around and around in her palms. She really *did* want to call on Mr. Vancouver, whether or not she asked him for his papers. She wanted to do it more than anything. She would rather be bitten by Nipper six times over than live another day with this throat-choking feeling of being ashamed of herself. Nipper's bites couldn't sting more than words like coward and baby.

Dorothy threw away the dandelion and scrambled to her feet. She would visit Mr. Vancouver right now! Even if she fainted from fright and had to be taken to the hospital in an ambulance!

She ran toward the broad fields and cherry orchards that belonged to Mr. Vancouver. Down the long, rutted driveway that led toward his out-buildings and farmhouse. Straight to Mr. Vancouver, who was just coming out of his barn with a pail of milk.

"Well for heaven's sake, child!" He set the pail down and hurried toward Dorothy. "Is something wrong at home?"

"No, sir." Dorothy licked her dry lips. "I just came—I just wondered—we're having a paper drive at school and I thought you might have some old newspapers?"

"Gracious," he said. "You're all lathered up. Does your mama know where you are? Have you got a handkerchief?" He pulled a huge, blue-and-red piece of cotton from a back pocket of his overalls and handed it to Dorothy. She wiped her face and stroked back her damp curls.

"Now, then," said Mr. Vancouver. "Let's just rest a minute till you catch your breath." He led the way to a fallen log and motioned Dorothy to sit alongside. He whistled for Nipper.

There was an answering yelp, a patter of feet, and the hound danced out of a field and up the driveway, his long ears flapping as he ran. Dorothy

flinched, but the dog scurried right past her and put his front paws into Mr. Vancouver's lap. The old man rubbed between Nipper's ears while Dorothy, watching, noticed the tan markings that came to a point on his forehead like a fashionable little widow's peak. Nipper was cute. And right now he didn't look at all fierce or dangerous, just happy to be loved.

"Now tell me again about the newspapers," said Mr. Vancouver after a moment. His voice was slow and gentle. And Dorothy found herself speaking quite easily about how badly the school needed a new piano and how angry Miss Cole would be if the fifth grade didn't help more.

Mr. Vancouver clucked with his tongue and shook his head regretfully. "So that's what's been going on! I just wish I had a nickel for every youngster who's stopped by in the last month. I'm so sorry, Dorothy, there's not a scrap of paper left on the place. I'd gladly have saved them all for you, but somehow I didn't expect you'd be by to ask."

"I meant to come sooner."

"Too bad you didn't." Mr. Vancouver rose and went to pick up his bucket of milk. "Do you want to help me feed the new calf?"

The sun was already touching the tips of the cherry trees. "I think I'd better go home now," said Dorothy. "It's almost suppertime."

"Well, then, come again another day."

"I will," said Dorothy, starting down the long driveway. She didn't know why it should be so, but making up her mind to come had been the hardest part of the visit.

CHAPTER TWELVE

Recital Day

The paper drive ended without any further contribution from Dorothy. She had wanted to turn in some more of Daddy's papers, but Mama claimed she needed them as much as the school did. Mama used part of the *Portland Oregonian* every morning when she lit the stove, and the rest of it for wrapping kitchen garbage.

The last day of school was only two weeks away now, and the fifth grade was deep in plans for its "Gifts to America" program. Pupils who had offered to take part often stayed after school to rehearse with Mrs. Merrick. At recess they gathered to talk importantly about the costumes their mothers were making, or the cookies their mothers would contribute. All parents had been invited to come watch the show and share in the refreshments that would follow.

Dorothy secretly yearned to be in the program, but Mrs. Merrick had not asked her and Dorothy was too bashful to volunteer. More than once these days Dorothy sat in her hiding place under the porch, imagining that she was dancing and singing along with the other children.

At home, life went along much as it had before the relatives came. Grandma was tiny and quiet and rarely left the house. She napped or knitted or helped Mama with housework, always shuffling about softly in a pair of old felt bedroom slippers. It was easy to forget that Grandma was around.

On the other hand, Uncle Max was often on Dorothy's mind, although she rarely saw him. He was always at work in Daddy's store or out studying with Mrs. Merrick or off in a corner with his nose in a book. He even ate supper ahead of the family so he could get to Mrs. Merrick's to mow her lawn or chop her kindling while it was still daylight. He did as many chores for Mrs. Merrick as he could, since she would not take money for her lessons.

Uncle Max had a proper haircut and American clothes now, and the hollows in his cheeks had already begun to fill out. He spoke better English every day. Dorothy wished earnestly to be his friend, but Uncle Max seldom spoke to her. She didn't know whether it was because he was too busy or because he was still mad at her. She thought it might help if she apologized for being a coward. She had the words all prepared in her head, but somehow the right moment to say them never came.

The biggest topic of conversation among the family these days was of leaving Woodburn. In the evenings, sitting on the porch after supper, Daddy was gradually convincing Mama that they ought to move to Portland.

At first Mama didn't want to talk about moving any place. She loved her home and she loved Woodburn and she hated changes. But Daddy returned to the subject over and over again. Finally Mama admitted that the house was indeed small for six people. It was a nuisance to keep house with Max sleeping in the parlor. Mama agreed with Daddy that Grandma was unhappy living in a town where there were no other Jewish families. Grandma would certainly be more contented if she could worship in a synagogue as she had done all her life.

Dorothy, listening quietly, was not really uneasy until the evening she heard Mama say, "All right, Avram, why don't you start looking at houses in Portland? But I hope you won't find a suitable place."

Dorothy hoped so, too. She would have worried a great deal about it if a more immediate concern was not looming directly ahead: the piano recital.

Every day brought the recital closer. Now Mama hurried to finish sewing Dorothy's new dress. Grandma spent hours embroidering a blue sash to go around it. Every afternoon Dorothy practiced the "Butterfly Waltz." She knew it by heart.

On the Friday before the recital, Miss Michaels was anxious. "Better play it through just once more," she said. "I want to make sure you've got this coda right." Miss Michaels jabbed her pencil at the passage which brought the piece to its concluding chord.

How could Mama still enjoy the "Butterfly Waltz"? She sat at her sewing table listening contentedly while Dorothy played the piece for the third time that afternoon. Mama's feet rocked the sewing machine treadle and her hands fed flat pieces of material into the flashing needle.

Dorothy came to the final coda. Her fingers hit

the last chord for the last time. Miss Michaels threw down her pencil and sighed, "Well, that will have to do. I'll see you tomorrow morning at the dress rehearsal." She stood to leave.

Mama came to the end of a seam and bit off the thread. The sewing machine had turned a long

straight strip of material into a frothy organdy ruffle. "I'm not sure about tomorrow morning," she said. "Saturday is Avram's busiest day and I hate to ask him to leave the store. And I don't know how I'll get this dress finished if I have to stop to take Dorothy to Portland. Is the rehearsal so important?"

"I think it would be well for Dorothy to run through the program with the other pupils," said Miss Michaels. "And of course she should see the stage at the Multnomah Hotel. If you like, I can take her myself tomorrow morning, but I'm driving up quite early."

"That would be very kind of you." Mama got up to escort Miss Michaels to the door. "Here, Dorothy, slip on this dress so I can mark the hem."

"I'll see you in the morning," Miss Michaels called from out in the front hall. "Please be ready promptly at eight."

Dorothy couldn't answer because she was already wriggling her way into the new dress, avoiding the pins that bristled in all directions. She heard the front door open and close.

"Climb up on this chair so I won't have to stoop," said Mama, returning to the parlor. She put a handful of pins into her mouth and began to stick them, one at a time, into the white organdy.

"This hem will be uneven if you don't stand straighter," Mama said after a short silence. "Why are you slumping so badly?"

Dorothy squared her shoulders. But it wasn't easy to stand tall when your throat throbbed and you felt like turning into nothing. Oh, how she dreaded tomorrow! Driving to Portland and back with Miss Michaels tomorrow morning was almost as bad as being in the recital tomorrow night.

As it turned out, Dorothy did not attend the dress rehearsal. She woke up with a sore throat. Mama put a wet compress around her neck and telephoned Miss Michaels. Dorothy could hear Miss Michaels' voice crackling out of the receiver.

"Yes, I'm sorry too," Mama replied. "But after all, what is there to rehearse? Dorothy knows the 'Butterfly Waltz' note by note. She's not really sick but I think she's better off at home."

So Dorothy spent the morning helping Anabelle make rose perfume. At least, Anabelle thought it would be rose perfume. "Don't you remember what happened when we tried it last year?" Dorothy asked, stroking a velvety petal. "The water turned slimy. And remember how it smelled? Ugh!"

"Maybe we made it wrong," Anabelle argued. "I don't see why we can't put a lot of petals into some water and let the smell steep out."

"This time let's use boiling water," Dorothy said. "We'll try making it exactly the way Mama makes tea."

The girls collected an assortment of bottles and jars. They washed and dried the containers, and filled them with fragrant red and yellow rose petals. They poured in boiling water. When the vessels were at last cool enough to handle, they moved them carefully to a board inside their hiding place.

Anabelle sniffed at the bottles. "How long will it take them to turn into perfume?"

"I guess we'll know by tomorrow." Dorothy sat down on the big rock and wished there were a magic way of getting to tomorrow without passing through today.

After lunch Mama asked Dorothy to nap, because she was going to be out later than usual that night. Dorothy went to her room and curled up obediently on her bed with Raggedy Ann. But her eyes would not close and her mind would not stop churning. She thought about a story she had read, by Edgar Allan Poe, about a man locked in a torture chamber. The walls of that room slowly closed in on the victim, forcing him into an abyss. So, too, was Dorothy being squeezed toward tonight. She was glad when Mama called upstairs to say there was enough hot water in the boiler now for Dorothy to take her bath.

Uncle Max and Dorothy ate an early supper together. As usual, Uncle Max read while he ate.

"Must you always have your nose in a book?" Mama complained.

"It's my lesson for tonight."

"You're not going to Mrs. Merrick's for a lesson tonight, are you?"

Uncle Max took his eyes from the book. "Why shouldn't I?"

"I expected you to come with us to Dorothy's recital," said Mama. "Don't you want to see your niece perform in public?"

"I forgot all about it," said Uncle Max. He looked across the table at Dorothy. "You'll excuse me. I care more for my studies than for piano-playing, you understand? I wish you good." He returned to his book and his food.

"If that's all the supper you're going to eat,

Dorothy, you might as well go upstairs and start dressing," said Mama. "I'll be up soon to brush your hair."

"I can brush my own hair."

"Of course," Mama said. "But tonight I'll do it. I want you to look extra pretty tonight."

Later, when Dorothy was all dressed and brushed and Mama was eating her own supper, Dorothy tiptoed into Mama's room. She wanted to take a look at herself in the triple mirrors of Mama's vanity table.

The mirrors showed three views of a beautiful new dress with crisp white ruffles. The blue taffeta hair ribbon exactly matched the wide embroidered sash, which was tied in a huge bow in back. The brown curls had never been neater. And yet the girl inside did not look pretty. She stared back from the mirrors with anxious eyes and pale cheeks. She had no dimples and probably never would have. But even dimples couldn't help the looks of a girl who felt as droopy as Dorothy.

A knot of discomfort formed in the pit of Dorothy's stomach. It lay there like a rock during the drive to Portland. Dorothy hardly heard what was said or noticed where they were as they drove through the rolling Oregon countryside. Her hands were wet and her throat was dry. All too soon the bright lights of Portland were ahead. The Moon crossed the bridge over the Willamette River and approached the Multnomah Hotel. To Dorothy the hotel was a towering, awesome structure, blazing with light.

Daddy let the family out at the main entrance and went off to park the car. Mama herded Grandma and the girls through an enormous lobby and along a passage to the recital hall. She left Anabelle and Grandma to find seats. She led Dorothy up some stairs and behind a curtain. There, backstage, they found Miss Michaels.

Miss Michaels was all dressed up in a beaded gown of iron gray. Her voice crackled with nervousness. She put a cold, wet palm on Dorothy's bare arm. "I'm glad you're here. I was beginning to worry."

Mama took Dorothy's coat. She fussed with the hair ribbon to make it stand up straighter. She untied and retied the bow of the sash. "There, that will do," she said. "Good luck, my darling." She kissed Dorothy and left to return to the auditorium.

Miss Michaels led Dorothy to a back corner where a dozen girls and one or two boys were standing about. "You're to wait here. And wait quietly, mind. I'll signal when it's your turn to go on stage." Miss Michaels bustled away.

"Isn't this exciting?" squeaked one of the girls. "I'm sure I'll be just awful!"

Dorothy found the edge of the backdrop. She gathered it aside so she could see into the hall. She stared as hard as she could, hunting for her family. There were a terrifying number of people sitting out there, and more coming down the aisles. She surveyed row after row of faces, none of them the familiar ones she sought.

Miss Michaels passed by and yanked Dorothy away from the edge of the curtain. "I told you to stay out of sight," she hissed. "Quiet, everybody! The recital is about to begin!"

CHAPTER THIRTEEN

Fighting the "Butterfly Waltz"

The lights in the hall dimmed. Miss Michaels pushed her first pupil out front to play. From backstage where the other performers waited their turn, the music sounded blurred. Miss Michaels cupped a hand behind her good ear and leaned against the curtain, straining to hear.

A series of girls, with now and then an unhappy boy, took their turn at the piano. Miss Michaels judged each performance by the amount of applause. If she heard only a scattering of claps, Miss Michaels merely nodded to the returning pupil. But when the approval from out front sounded louder or longer than usual, Miss Michaels tapped the victorious pianist on the arm and said, "Well done," or "I'm proud of you."

Meanwhile the pupils waiting backstage eddied

about, whispering to one another and trying to muffle their giggles. Only Dorothy stood alone, lost in her fog of fear. Suddenly Miss Michaels gripped her elbow, steered her to an opening in the curtain, gave her a little shove and said, "You're on!"

Dorothy found herself standing high on a stage in front of ten million people.

She stood blinking, looking for the piano. Almost blind with fright, she dimly saw an instrument shaped like the old upright at home. As she tottered toward it she thought she heard Mama's voice somewhere far away. Mama seemed to be calling, "No!"

Dorothy sat down at the instrument. She hitched the stool closer to the keyboard and shaped her fingers to strike the opening notes of the "Butterfly Waltz."

She touched the keys. Not a sound came out. Surprised, Dorothy struck again, a little harder. Her fingernails clicking against the ivory made the only noise in the absolutely silent auditorium.

The keys felt strange. Dorothy looked and saw there were two rows of keys on this small, odd instrument. A piano had only one.

Dorothy looked wildly about her for a real

piano. This time she saw the concert grand, placed way up at the front of the stage. It was shaped like an enormous black bird with a lifted wing.

As Dorothy rose from the organ the silence was total. Followed by rows and rows of eyes, she walked stiffly over to the concert grand. She sat at the keyboard. Once more she brought her fingers down in the opening notes of the "Butterfly Waltz." This piano worked.

Dorothy forced her hands through the notes of the waltz. They jerked on and on. Before she knew it she had played past the final coda and started again. There was no help for it, Dorothy had to run through the "Butterfly Waltz" for the second time.

Her fingers moved mechanically as her mind raced ahead, trying to remember the ending. She squeezed her eyes shut to help bring back the notes of the sheet music. But she couldn't visualize the notes, only Miss Michaels' black pencil marks splattered over the pages. Dorothy found herself at the beginning of the "Butterfly Waltz" for the third time.

It was horrible. She might play the "Butterfly Waltz" forever. She broke off abruptly, hesitated a moment and then struck the final chord. She put her trembling hands in her lap and sat for an instant of breathless silence. Then the audience burst into tremendous applause. They were clapping because they felt sorry for her.

Miss Michaels, waiting on the other side of the curtain with her hand behind her ear, misunderstood the noise. "You must have played exceptionally well," she whispered when Dorothy appeared backstage. "Better take another bow." She pushed Dorothy back onto the stage. Dorothy gave a jerky little curtsy to another round of applause. Then, numb with misery, she was allowed to retire to a dark backstage corner.

After a time Miss Michaels waved all the pupils onto the stage to take one last group bow. A little girl came running up the aisle with a big basket of red roses for the teacher. There was more clapping. People began crowding around the performers, congratulating Miss Michaels and claiming their children. The concert was over.

Daddy and Mama came up and kissed Dorothy. Grandma kissed her too, murmuring some words of comfort in Russian. "When we get home, I'll give you my jacks," whispered Anabelle. She put her hand in Dorothy's and they all walked out of the auditorium, out of the Multnomah Hotel, into the cool, dark evening.

Daddy had parked the Moon near an ice cream parlor called The Pig N'Whistle. A pink-and-green painted pig danced a jig on the wooden sign over the door. He was playing the hornpipe. Through the plate-glass windows of the shop Dorothy saw people eating sundaes and drinking sodas as though nothing had happened.

"Shall we stop in for a banana split?" asked Daddy.

But for the first time in her life Dorothy could not eat ice cream. That lump in her stomach left room for nothing else. "I want to go home," she said.

They got into the car and drove out of Portland in silence. Nobody spoke until they were halfway to Woodburn. Then Mama said, "Somebody should complain to the management. Why did they have to leave a harmonium on the stage?"

"It isn't the management's fault," said Daddy. "After all, they had it pushed way to the back of the platform."

"Yes, Dorothy, what ever possessed you to go to that organ? Didn't you hear me calling you?"

"Don't blame the child, Jennie," said Daddy sharply. "If she'd been to the dress rehearsal with the others she'd have known the layout, too."

"Is it my fault she missed the dress rehearsal?" snapped Mama.

Dorothy shivered. She seldom heard her parents quarrel.

They drove again in uncomfortable silence. This time when Mama spoke she said, "Apart from this evening, I've felt that Dorothy isn't coming along with the piano as well as she should. I've half a mind to look around for another teacher."

"There's no need for another teacher. Miss Michaels has nothing to do with it."

"What do you mean?"

"You know well enough what I mean. You just don't want to understand."

"Are you blaming me for something?" Mama asked in a harsh voice.

"No, I suppose it's my own fault," said Daddy. "I should have stopped this piano-lesson nonsense long ago. The unvarnished truth is that Dorothy is not a musician and she'll never be one. You know, you can lead a horse to water but you can't make him drink."

"Avram!" Mama sounded horrified. "Do you compare your daughter to a horse? Do you want her to grow up here in America like I did in

Russia? Ignorant, without accomplishments of any kind?" Mama was so upset she was almost choking.

Dorothy, her eyes closed, listened in misery from the back seat. She was the cause of these angry words between her parents. For as far back as she could remember, she had failed in everything she ever tried to do. She was nothing but a disappointment to everybody. Dorothy tried to hold back her tears, but they slid out through her closed eyelids and fell off the peaks of her cheeks.

When Daddy spoke again, it was in a gentler tone. "I know you have this dream for our children, otherwise I'd have spoken up long ago. But Jennie, dearest, a child isn't a loaf of bread. You can't shape her to your will. Let's be grateful she's healthy and smart and good-hearted. So what if she can't play the piano? Maybe when she grows up she'll be able to bake bread as good as yours. Isn't that an accomplishment, too, to give happiness to her family?"

Mama didn't answer and they completed the trip in silence. Dorothy hurried to undress and tumble into bed. She could hardly wait for Anabelle to put out the light so she could curl up in the darkness with old Raggedy Ann.

Anabelle quickly fell asleep but Dorothy was

still lying awake when, much later, Mama tiptoed into the room. She tucked the blankets up tight around each girl's shoulders. She found the new dress lying across the foot of Dorothy's bed and put it on a hanger in the closet. She opened the windows and adjusted the blinds. Then she came and stood near Dorothy's bed.

Mama stood in the darkness for a long time. At last she sighed, the deepest longest sigh Dorothy had ever heard, and said under her breath, "May God forgive me. How can a mother know a child's soul?"

She tiptoed to the head of Dorothy's bed and whispered, "Are you awake?" Dorothy stirred. Mama leaned over. She pressed her soft lips to Dorothy's forehead.

"No more piano lessons," she said. "Now sleep in peace."

CHAPTER FOURTEEN

Dorothy Meets a Prince

Dorothy awoke to a sunny Sunday morning, rich with the smell of frying doughnuts. She lay still a moment trying to remember last night. But it was impossible to summon up feelings of unhappiness in the presence of such a mouth-watering odor. Dorothy hurried into her clothes, splashed a handful of water over her face, and followed the scent to the kitchen.

Mama was at the stove, lifting crisp brown doughnuts out of a kettle of oil. Anabelle stood by the wooden drainboard cutting crazy shapes out of odds and ends of dough.

"Good morning, Dorothy," said Mama, forking a hot drained doughnut into a bath of powdered sugar. She spoke as though last night had never happened. "Breakfast is ready as soon as I finish up that last sheet of dough. Will you cut it for me?"

Dorothy used a sharp tin cutter to punch out the round doughnut shapes. Mama picked up each one and slipped it carefully into the bubbling oil. Dorothy stood beside her, watching as the doughnuts swelled up big and brown. As they cooked, the flat inside circles turned into the puffy round balls which Dorothy called holes. When Mama flipped them over to fry their second sides, these holes floated gently away from the mother doughnuts.

"Can I fry mine now?" asked Anabelle. "Look, this one's going to be a lizard!"

"Let me put them in the oil for you, I don't want you to burn yourself," said Mama. "Dorothy, do you want to make yourself some animals too?"

"I still like holes best."

"All right then. Call the men. Where's Grandma?" Mama put a heaping platter of doughnuts on the table and poured coffee for the grown-ups.

The family gathered. Dorothy had eaten an uncounted number of holes when Daddy, dipping a doughnut into his coffee, asked, "Who wants to come to Portland with us? There's a house out on Sandy Boulevard I'd like to show you."

"It's certainly a lovely day for a ride," said

Mama, glancing out the window. "My pot roast is all cooked, so dinner's ready whenever we get home."

"Do I have to go?" asked Dorothy.

"I suppose not," said Daddy. "But if you come, I'll buy you an ice cream cone at The Pig N'Whistle. How about you, Max?"

"Not I," said Max.

"Aw, come on," Anabelle urged Dorothy. "We can take the jacks along and we'll have ice cream and everything."

But Dorothy finished chewing her last round, crusty little hole and said, "I'm tired of going to Portland. I'd rather stay home and read."

Dorothy sat on the front steps with *The Purple Book of Fairy Tales* in her lap. She waved good-by to Daddy and Mama and Grandma and Anabelle. When the Moon had disappeared up the road she opened her book and tried to read. But this June day demanded to be noticed. The tree by the gate was covered with tiny green apples and the rose bushes at the side of the house were a swaggering row of red and yellow blossoms. Fleecy white clouds chased across the sky. It was a day for doing something.

Dorothy put down the book and wandered rest-
lessly around the yard. She remembered the rose
perfume and decided to check up on it. She
squeezed through the lattice and into the familiar
hiding place. Picking up one of the jars, she held it
to the light and studied the cloudy green water.
She sniffed critically. The water didn't quite stink
but it scarcely smelled like Mama's perfume,
either. She and Anabelle would have to wait another day to see how their experiment was working.
But it didn't look promising.

Dorothy was about to crawl out of the opening when she heard the noise of Uncle Max's bicycle coming around from the back of the house. She waited quietly and watched as Uncle Max, eating a doughnut, cycled out of the yard and off in the direction of Mrs. Merrick's house. Then she crept back into the sunshine and sat down once more on the front step.

Dorothy fell to musing about Uncle Max. She wished there were some way of telling him, without words, how much she wanted to be friends. She noticed the book of fairy tales and gave it a push that sent it spinning across the porch. It was all very well in fairy tales, where people could slay dragons or summon genies to do their bidding. But in real life there weren't any dragons.

Out of the corner of an eye Dorothy caught a slight movement at the gate. She jumped up, startled. A big white dog was trying to come in! How had he sneaked up so quietly? Thank goodness the gate was closed. Her heart beat a little faster as she wondered if the dog could jump over the fence.

But as she watched him, even Dorothy could see that there was nothing fierce about this dog. He didn't growl or bark or show any intention of jumping or biting. He stared at Dorothy out of mild brown eyes and waved his plumed tail.

Dorothy walked toward the gate for a closer look, and the dog took a few steps back. He kept his eyes on her face and his tail wagged with such eagerness that his whole body wagged with it. Dorothy hadn't realized a dog could be so friendly. And smart, too. How did he know that he should stand back so she could open the gate?

She unlatched the gate and the dog walked in. She walked up the path with the dog right beside her. She sat down on the steps and he put his long nose across Dorothy's knees, just begging to be petted. She timidly scratched behind his ears and he immediately craned his neck forward so that every possible inch of skin could be rubbed.

Dorothy stroked the dog more boldly now, between the ears and under his lovely long chin. She felt carefully through his thick white hair for some evidence of ownership but he wore no collar. For all she knew, he might have stepped out of the pages of the fairy tale book. The dog had such an aristocratic nose and such deep, soft brown eyes. It was easy to imagine a human being inside. Perhaps this dog was a person in disguise, maybe a handsome young prince under the spell of a witch.

"Here, Prince!" Dorothy said, leaping to her feet and running around the yard. "Come, Prince!"

Prince followed closely. When Dorothy stopped, he stopped. She sat down cross-legged on the grass and he lay beside her. This was no ordinary dog.

Dorothy was sitting blissfully in the sunshine, her arm on the dog's neck, when a great idea came to her: Even if she had never heard Uncle Max say so, she was sure he would love to own a dog. What if she kept Prince now, and gave him to Uncle Max when he came home? Of course she would have to play with Prince and take care of him whenever Uncle Max was away. That was the best part of this best idea. Through Prince, she and Uncle Max would be friends!

Excited by her plan, Dorothy began to train Prince at once. She threw a stick and he fetched it back. She climbed up into the apple tree and Prince put his forepaws on the trunk and tried to climb up too. What a wonderful dog!

At that moment Prince turned away from the apple tree and trotted toward the open front gate. "Here, Prince! Come back!" called Dorothy as she scrambled out of the tree. She ran to the gate and closed it in Prince's face.

While she held a restraining arm around Prince's

neck, Dorothy racked her brains for a way to explain that he lived here now. I'll give him something to eat! she thought. She dimly remembered reading that a dog will always stay where he has been fed.

Half pulling and half guiding Prince, Dorothy led him around to the back door. Then she remembered that Mama didn't permit dogs in the house because she said they carried germs. Oh well, thought Dorothy, Prince could live outdoors and sleep in the tool shed. "Wait here!" she told him. "Don't go away! I'll be right back!"

She hurried into the house and threw open the door of the cooler. What should she offer Prince? Peanut butter? No. What else was in the cooler then? She pushed containers aside as she rejected rice, eggs, carrots, cheese. Nothing a dog would like.

She dashed to the pantry to check the contents of the wooden icebox. Here, too, was disappointment: Butter. Lettuce. Chicken soup. Nothing to appeal to a beautiful Prince.

Hurry, hurry, she thought. He might go away.

Dorothy's eyes toured the clean, quiet kitchen and came to rest on a black iron kettle standing at the back of the stove. She ran to the kettle, tipped the lid and peered inside. Pot roast! The very thing to enslave a dog forever. Without losing a moment she picked up the warm pot roast and carried it dripping across the kitchen, through the pantry and out the back door.

Prince was gone.

"Prince! Prince!" With both hands clutching the pot roast Dorothy ran wildly around the side of the house. Prince, she saw, was out in the road. He paused when he heard Dorothy calling. She raced to him and threw the meat down before him.

Prince sniffed the roast and turned away. Dorothy fastened her arms around his neck and dragged him back to the food. "Eat!" she said, pushing his face down.

Prince gave the pot roast a few dainty licks. Then, wagging his tail as though to say, "Sorry, my dear," he trotted off down the road.

Dorothy stared down at the pot roast. For the first time she wondered what Mama would say when she got home. The fever of dog ownership drained from her and she wished she had not been so quick to seize the family's dinner. Well, there was no help for it now. The meat was covered with dust and besides it had been licked by a dog.

Dorothy picked up the pot roast and carried it

back to the kitchen. She wrapped it neatly in newspaper, as she had seen Mama do a thousand times
with spoiled food. She took the bundle outside and
deposited it gently inside the garbage can. She was
back in the kitchen, straightening the jars and
bottles disarranged in her mad flight through the
cooler, when the telephone rang. Two longs and
a short.

CHAPTER FIFTEEN

Mr. Vancouver's Recipe

Dorothy recognized the quiet voice that answered her hello. She said, "Daddy isn't home, Mr. Vancouver."

"No, no, it's not your daddy I'm calling. It's you I want. Will you ask your mama to let you come over here after dinner?"

"Mama isn't home. I could come right now," Dorothy offered. "Why?"

"I have something to show you," said Mr. Vancouver.

"A newborn calf?"

"I'm not telling over the phone, but you can come now if you like. I'll be out in the garden."

It was a long walk to Mr. Vancouver's farm. Dorothy had plenty of time to think, but as she hurried along she couldn't imagine what it was he wanted to show her. Something special, certainly, for Mr. Vancouver had never asked her to come over before. But then, she never would have gone before, either. Dorothy broke into a hippety-hop kind of skip. It was nice to be going away from home all by herself like this, not feeling the least bit timid.

She found Mr. Vancouver kneeling in his garden, hammering stakes into the ground alongside a row of young tomato plants. When he saw Dorothy coming up the long driveway he pulled himself to his feet and wiped his soiled hands on the front of his overalls. From somewhere in the orchard Nipper began barking furiously; another moment and he was streaking toward Dorothy.

As naturally as though she had always known how to handle dogs, Dorothy crouched to meet the eager little beagle. He danced around, sniffing and licking her outstretched fingers. Dorothy patted him and wondered at the silliness of any-body being afraid of a dog like Nipper.

"So you've made friends with him, have you?" Mr. Vancouver hobbled toward her, one hand holding a stiff hip. "He loves young people to frisk and bounce with him. I'm not so good in that line any more. Come along, let's go on up to the barn." He led the way toward the faded red structure at the far end of the driveway.

Inside the rickety building, with its floor of hard-packed earth, were rows of stalls for Mr. Vancouver's horses and his half-dozen cows. The stables were empty now; at this time of day all the animals were out grazing in the meadow.

Dorothy looked about in the dusty half-light. Every inch of wall and floor was crammed with the equipment that collects on a farm: ropes and rakes and hoes and plows and saddles and rows of milk buckets hanging on nails near a water pump. Mr. Vancouver's wagon was parked inside the barn, too, its empty shafts drooping downward. The buggy looked lonesome without a horse hitched in front.

Nowhere did Dorothy see anything that looked like a surprise for her.

Mr. Vancouver leaned against the open doorway with his thumbs hooked through his overall straps, clearly enjoying his mystery. All the wrinkles in his face seemed to light up when he smiled. After a time he motioned with his forefinger and led Dorothy to the side of the wagon.

She was not tall enough to see inside. Mr. Vancouver cupped his hands under her elbows, grunted

"Ally oop!" and hoisted her up for an instant.
Dorothy saw newspapers.

On the second lift she saw a whole wagon full.
The third time, forgetting the danger of getting
axle grease on her dress, she grabbed the rim of the
wagon wheel and climbed the spokes for a good

long look. Yes, it was true. The wagon contained stacks and stacks of newspapers. As many as she had collected in any daydream.

Dorothy gasped with surprise. "Where did you ever find so many papers?"

Mr. Vancouver grinned as wide as a Halloween pumpkin. "The hardest part was finding the time to drive to Portland. Getting the papers was easy— I just asked my nephew for them. You see, my sister's boy is a printer at the *Portland Oregonian*. He was glad to help out when I told him about the school's paper drive."

"Oh!" Dorothy's face fell. "It's too late! The paper drive ended last week."

"Ended, did it? Too bad. I'd been meaning to get up to Portland ever since you came round here asking for papers so nicely. But it isn't easy for me to leave the farm for a whole day." Mr. Vancouver walked out into the sunshine, Nipper at his heels.

"Thanks just the same," said Dorothy, following. "It was awfully nice of you."

"My pleasure." Mr. Vancouver leaned against the barn siding. "To tell the truth, I wanted to give Miss Cole a little boost, too. She's had a hard life, that woman, and she's given eighteen years of it to Woodburn School with little thanks that I can see. Come to think of it, why don't you just go ahead and ask Miss Cole if she'll take these papers, late or no? I've never known her to turn down anything yet if it'll do her precious school any good."

A chill rippled up Dorothy's spine. The thought of knocking on that ominous glass-paneled door marked "Principal's Office" made her feel weak in the knees. "Couldn't you please ask her, Mr. Vancouver?"

Nipper settled down for a nap. Mr. Vancouver watched as the dog turned in circles and then curled up alongside the barn and closed his eyes. "I guess I *could*." Mr. Vancouver drummed the fingers of his right hand across his cheek while he considered the proposition. After some moments he looked down at the beseeching face still turned up to his.

"But I'd like to try to give you another gift, Dorothy," he said abruptly. "This one is more valuable than newspapers. I wasn't so much older than you when I first stumbled onto it."

"What?" asked Dorothy.

"I figured it out one night in a muddy ditch when I was fighting in the Civil War. I've always called it a recipe for courage."

Mr. Vancouver headed slowly down the driveway toward the garden, and Dorothy followed him. "If you're full of fears, you're no different from anybody else," he began in his gentle voice. "I don't suppose there's a creature on earth who lives without fear. In a way, it doesn't matter whether the terror is about death on a battlefield or shadows dancing on a wall, because the recipe for courage is the same. A brave person is just an ordinary soul like you or me who decides he wants to face his fears and control them. Do you understand what I mean?"

Mr. Vancouver stepped over the wire fence that kept the rabbits and woodchucks out of his garden. "Come back soon and play with Nipper," he said.

Dorothy waved good-by and started thoughtfully home. She walked slowly, placing each shoe directly in front of the other so her footprints would show in one straight line. For a time she walked backwards in order to see the shapes she made in the dust of the road.

All the while she was thinking about Mr. Vancouver's recipe. What if she did knock on the door of the principal's office tomorrow morning? Dorothy imagined Miss Cole opening the door and staring coldly down at her, as she had at Uncle

Max. "If this is some kind of a joke, I am not amused!" said the Miss Cole inside Dorothy's head, and she slammed the door.

Dorothy trudged forward. Wouldn't it be brave enough just to write Miss Cole a note? She could do it tonight, and check every single word in Daddy's dictionary to make sure nothing was misspelled. But then how would she deliver the note? What if Miss Cole swooped out of her office just as Dorothy was pushing the note under her door? Dorothy shivered and abandoned the note.

Suddenly Dorothy had a fine idea, the best one of all. She stopped in her tracks and drew a deep breath of relief. She would simply ask Mrs. Merrick to tell Miss Cole about the papers. Why hadn't she thought of Mrs. Merrick before? Dorothy turned around. She would go back to Mrs. Merrick's house and ask her right this minute.

As Dorothy wheeled about she noticed she was standing on the corner where Miss Cole's lane joined Main Street. A horse and buggy clopped up the narrow side road and waited for a Ford to pass before it turned cautiously into the main street.

Dorothy waited too, and as she stood there an image of Uncle Max's face flashed into her mind. What would Uncle Max say if he knew she had to beg for help like this? Dorothy ducked her head to avoid the words she all but heard Uncle Max throw at her: "Coward! Baby!"

As she teetered on the corner. Dorothy was no longer conscious of the passing traffic. Inside herself she was standing on another kind of corner and she had to make her choice. Which way?

Taking in a gulp of breath with a sound like a sob, Dorothy began to run.

CHAPTER SIXTEEN

Dorothy Chooses

Dorothy never remembered twisting the doorbell or hearing it ring. But she must have done so, for once again the dog inside set up a fearful barking. Dorothy edged back toward the porch steps.

Miss Cole seemed surprised when she opened the door. She said something Dorothy couldn't hear over the wild yapping of the dog. "Hush!" said Miss Cole louder and then, "Wait a minute, please!" to Dorothy. She disappeared from the door. Dorothy heard a scrabbling noise from the dog's nails as he was pulled across a wooden floor. A distant door slammed. Miss Cole reappeared.

"I don't know why I put up with that animal," she said sharply. "Now, then, would you like to come in, Dorothy? The dog won't hurt you, he's shut up in the kitchen."

Dorothy shook her head. She preferred not to enter the dim unknown of Miss Cole's house. It was a surprise that Miss Cole knew her name. In all five years at Woodburn School, Dorothy had never once talked to the principal. That was because only those pupils who misbehaved were sent to Miss Cole's office. Edgar Lemon, for instance, had spoken with Miss Cole many times.

"Then I'll just step outside," said Miss Cole. "I've been cleaning house all morning and I could use a breath of air."

Miss Cole was wearing an ordinary apron like Mama's. Dorothy had never thought of Miss Cole as a person who might wear an apron and perform familiar household chores of dusting and sweeping.

The principal pulled up a wooden chair and plopped onto it with a sigh of weariness. "Well, now, what is it?" she said, and Dorothy realized Miss Cole spoke in a sharp tone even when she wasn't cross. It was just the kind of voice she had. Yet it was a stopping kind of voice, not easy to talk to.

Dorothy faced Miss Cole. "I—" she began. "The paper drive—"

"That paper drive again? I begin to think it's like the dog, more trouble than it's worth. Take

your time, now, and tell me what you have to say about the paper drive."

Helped along by questions from Miss Cole, Dorothy managed to explain about Uncle Max and Mr. Vancouver and the papers now waiting in Mr. Vancouver's wagon.

"Well, well," said Miss Cole, and then, "Did

Mr. Vancouver mention how many pounds he has?"

"No, but there are lots and lots of papers."

"If there should be about two thousand pounds it would just make the difference," said Miss Cole. "I've had a piano all picked out for months now, but the paper drive fell short and I thought we'd just have to wait another year. It was quite a disappointment to me because the school needs a new piano desperately." Miss Cole got up. "I'll go telephone Mr. Vancouver right this minute. There's no sense pretending I'm not interested in those papers."

Dorothy, feeling dismissed, started down the stairs.

"Oh, Dorothy, one moment," called Miss Cole, stopping with one hand on her doorknob. "As you know, our paper drive is over. Miss Tipton's seventh grade won the prize. It wouldn't be fair to change that now, you realize."

"Yes, ma'am."

"Very well. Thank you ever so much for your help." Miss Cole's door almost closed, then opened again. "Please thank Max, too. Tell him I regret my misunderstanding." The door clicked shut.

Dorothy danced off down the road, feeling light

as a ball of dandelion seeds drifting along on a breeze. She had done it, she had turned that corner!

As she floated back to Main Street she saw Uncle Max cycling toward her. "Uncle Max!" she yelled, raising a hand to stop him. "Can I have a ride?"

Uncle Max looked surprised. He braked his bicycle and skidded to a stop. "All right," he said. "Hurry up. Hungry I am enough to eat the Kremlin. I hope we have the dinner soon."

The dinner! The dog! The pot roast! Mama! Remembrance swept over Dorothy. She covered her face with her hands and rocked back and forth on her feet. "Oh-oh! Am I going to catch sixty!"

Uncle Max said, "What is it, then? Tell me, maybe I help?"

He laughed when she told him. Dorothy didn't consider her trouble funny, but it was nice to see Uncle Max laughing.

"Jump on," he said. "We waste time."

Dorothy got on the bicycle bar in front of Uncle Max. Off they rode, so fast that Dorothy's hair blew straight out behind.

"Hold please your curls, they blow into my face," said Uncle Max.

It was fun to go skimming along, one hand

behind her head and the other holding tight to the bicycle. As they approached Enid Stidd's house, Dorothy saw that Enid was again sitting in front.

Enid jumped up and ran to meet them. "Please, now can I have a ride?"

"No time," puffed Uncle Max.

"Later, then?" Enid begged as she ran alongside. Gradually falling behind, she called, "Can I come over to your house?"

Dorothy wiped a curl out of her mouth. At the risk of tumbling off, she let go of the bicycle long enough to turn around and yell back, "This afternoon!"

Enid dropped away. Uncle Max pedaled on through Main Street. They whizzed past the variety shop, the livery stables, the butcher shop and the post office, the drug store and Daddy's hardware shop. There were no cars parked at the curb today, no horses hitched to the posts. A Sunday quiet lay over Woodburn.

Uncle Max steered around a corner, the bicycle dipping dangerously to one side. Dorothy, craning her neck to look ahead, reported, "They're not home yet. But what difference does that make? What can we do?"

"We think of something," replied Max.

When the family returned from Portland half an hour later they found Uncle Max adding coal to the stove. Potatoes boiled in a kettle and Dorothy had just begun to set the table.

"Good!" said Daddy. "We're all starving."

Mama removed her hat and put on her apron. "What wonderful children you are, so thoughtful!" Mama picked up a fork and tested the pot roast. "We'll be ready to sit down in no time. Mmm, the meat smells good."

Mama bustled about completing the preparations for dinner, her voice as bubbly as the cooking potatoes. "Oh, did we see a house!" She took a head of lettuce from the icebox and handed it to Grandma, who began to prepare a salad. "You won't believe how beautiful, with a gas range in the kitchen! No more lighting a fire every morning in this old stove. No more kindling and newspapers and dirty coal. All I'll have to do is strike a match and turn on the gas jet. I never dreamed life could be so easy!"

"Are we going to move?" Dorothy asked.

"I hope so," said Daddy, who was already seated at the table waiting for his dinner. "You'll like the new house, Dorothy. It's way out on Sandy Boulevard, only a few blocks inside the city limits. There's a meadow across the street and a woods right behind our back yard. In a way, that house is more in the country than this one."

"Where's the high school?" asked Uncle Max. "Can I ride there on my bike?"

"You'll have to take the streetcar, Max. Lincoln High is on the other side of the river."

"The girls are going to have a long walk to their school." Mama was slicing pot roast now. "About fifteen blocks. That's one thing I don't like about the new house. Sandy Boulevard is such a busy street to cross, and besides I don't think the children should go so far from home alone."

"Now, Jennie, not again," said Daddy. "Unless you want the girls to go through life holding your hand, you've got to believe they can take care of themselves."

Mama sighed. "Yes, I know. I guess it's my nature to worry. Come, everybody, dinner's ready."

Anabelle, who had been sitting unnoticed on the floor in a corner of the kitchen, burst into tears. "I don't want to move to Portland," she announced. She threw away the little red ball she had been playing jacks with. It bounced against a wall and rolled under the table. "I don't like any new school! I don't even know where it is! I'll get lost!"

Daddy made a move to comfort Anabelle, but it was Dorothy who got there first. On her knees, she leaned forward and put her arms around her little sister. "Don't worry, Anabelle," she said softly. "You can walk to school with me every single day. After a while you'll probably have some friends of your own. You'll see, everything is going to be all right."

"Wipe your nose, Anabelle, and wash your hands." Mama sat down to her heaping plate of food. "I hope the ice cream cone didn't spoil your appetite."

But it was Dorothy, not Anabelle, who picked at her dinner. She still saw vividly how the meat had looked when Uncle Max first fished it out of the garbage can, dusty and swarming with red ants. Uncle Max had washed it before replacing it in the pot, but even so . . . Dorothy studied her gravy carefully for floating bodies.

"What's the matter, dear, why don't you eat?" asked Mama. "Maybe the meat needs another pinch of salt?" She sprinkled her own serving and passed the salt cellar over to Dorothy.

"The meat is delicious," Uncle Max said emphatically, looking directly at Dorothy. "Is nothing wrong. In Russia, where people are hungry, they dream of so wonderful food like this." He carried a huge forkful of meat to his mouth.

"But Uncle Max, what if they knew the meat had been all smeared with dust and ants and germs from a dog? What if it came up out of a garbage can, would people eat it just the same?"

"Dorothy, this is not proper table talk," said Mama. "Really, I don't know where your ideas come from."

But Uncle Max said seriously, "When people truly starve they look to eat dogs, rats, anything." He looked across the table at Dorothy and added with a wink, "In emergency times comes different actions."

Dorothy chewed a tiny bit of pot roast and mashed potatoes. After a moment, she winked back.

CHAPTER SEVENTEEN

The Secret

The following day Dorothy asked Mama for permission to go with Uncle Max when he visited Mrs. Merrick that evening.

"Of course you can go, if Max doesn't mind," said Mama. "But what is there for you to do at Mrs. Merrick's house while she teaches Max? Won't you just be in the way?"

"It's a secret," said Dorothy. "Please don't ask me any questions."

In the succeeding days she managed to keep her secret, in spite of Anabelle's steady attempts to ferret it out. Anabelle was wildly curious to know what was making Dorothy so busy and so excited. "Will you tell me if I guess right? Does it have something to do with school?"

"I won't tell."

"Then I'll never tell you anything," said Anabelle, "not unless you give me *two* rides when Enid comes."

For Enid came over almost every afternoon now. She and Dorothy were helping one another learn to ride Max's bicycle. Poor Anabelle, her legs were too short even to reach the blocks Uncle Max had tied around the pedals, so she was reduced to wheedling rides from the big girls. She sat proudly on the leather seat, her feet dangling uselessly, while Dorothy and Enid pushed the bicycle around the block. Then Anabelle could only watch while the other two took turns wobbling unsteadily back and forth in front of the house. When Anabelle complained, Dorothy borrowed a page from Mama's book. "Your turn will come," she said.

And then suddenly it was Friday, June nineteenth, the last day of school. Dorothy hopped out of bed the moment her eyes were open and dressed herself with special care. She took the delicate white organdy dress off its hanger in the closet and slipped it on over her head. She had trouble with her sash until she decided to tie it in front, where it was easy to get at. Then she slid the sash around until the big fat bow was in the middle of her back where it belonged.

Dorothy went into Mama's room to look at herself in the long mirror. When she whirled around, the crisp ruffles floated wide as a ballerina's skirt. Dorothy sat on the bench in front of Mama's vanity table. She stuck her face close to the center mirror and angled the two side mirrors inward until she saw herself reflected over and over again, fifteen happy faces of Dorothy.

She ran to the kitchen, where the other members of the family were already at breakfast. Daddy put down his cereal spoon and whistled. "My, what a pretty girl! Your eyes are as blue as your sash."

"Why are you wearing your best dress? You're not in the program," said Anabelle.

"I'm glad you like the dress," Mama said. "Might as well use it before you grow out of it, but you'd better wear a napkin this morning." Mama tied a huge dishtowel around Dorothy's neck as insurance against eggs on the dress.

"Are you coming to school this morning, for sure?" she asked Mama.

"Of course I'm coming. Grandma, too. Mrs. Merrick especially asked Grandma to bake some spice cookies for the refreshments. Grandma's so pleased." Grandma, sitting at the table with black coffee, smiled and nodded. She understood quite a lot of English now, although she rarely spoke except in Yiddish or Russian.

"Will you visit my room, too?" Anabelle asked.

"If there's time. But Mrs. Merrick asked us first."

"Not fair," grumbled Anabelle.

"Your turn will come," said Mama soothingly. "I'll leave some cookies for your class in any case. Goodness knows, Grandma made enough for an army."

"Remember, don't be late," Dorothy said when she kissed Mama good-by. "Eleven o'clock."

"You *are* excited! I'll bet Anabelle's right, you're going to read a poem?"

Dorothy smiled and refused to answer.

Enid was in the schoolyard, dressed as an English shepherdess in a long flowered skirt with a green bodice. The colors made her hair look blacker and her skin whiter than ever.

"Hey, you look pretty!" Enid came charging up as Dorothy entered. "I wish I had hair the color of yours. It looks like pulled taffy. Say, how come you're all dressed up when you're not in the program?"

Miss Cole appeared at the door of the school with the big brass bell in her hand. She shook it vigorously. Children poured out of every corner of the yard to gather in front of the steps. Latecomers heard the bell a block away and raced down the road.

"Are you?" persisted Enid as the girls took their places in the line that was forming.

But Dorothy only smiled.

This last morning in school was not like other days. People turned in their books and cleaned out their desks and washed down the blackboards. They talked about summer plans.

Ozro Marschner said he was going to visit a circus in Seattle, and when he was older he was going to join a circus.

Ruby Visceglia reported that she and Emerald were going to stay with an aunt, all summer long. Their aunt lived far away in Yreka, California. The girls would get there on a Southern Pacific train.

Dorothy impulsively raised her voice and told the class she was going to move to Portland.

"I wish I could move some place," muttered Edgar Lemon. "Nothing ever happens in this burg."

Now parents began to arrive. Mrs. Merrick ushered them to chairs which had been placed around three sides of the room. Mrs. Merrick's desk was squeezed back into a corner to make a space for the performers.

Three boys ran out to fetch the brand-new school piano that rolled easily on ball-bearing wheels. It was a small, low piano made of pretty light-brown wood, with a keyboard the same as the one at home.

In spite of herself, Dorothy's heart was thudding. Mama and Grandma came in. Mrs. Merrick greeted them at the door and introduced them to some other grown-ups. They were both dressed up and Grandma was not wearing her bedroom slippers.

Shortly the classroom was buzzing with parents. Mrs. Merrick called for attention. The room fell silent and the program began.

From a distance, Dorothy heard Mrs. Merrick play the new piano while Kitty McCloskey sang an Irish folk tune. Ruby and Emerald performed their Italian peasant dance and Enid recited an English ballad. Dorothy sat quietly as the program went on. Whenever she heard clapping she clapped, too, but she felt far away.

Out of the warm blackness around her came Mrs. Merrick's voice: "The final number on our program has been a well-kept secret. Dorothy will tell you about it herself."

A familiar numbness seized Dorothy. She was afraid her legs would crumble if she stood up. She squeezed her eyes shut for a moment. The room was very quiet.

When she opened her eyes again the blackness was gone. Mrs. Merrick, standing up front, was looking at her with anxious concern. Mama leaned forward in her chair. Her hands were gripped together in her lap and she was biting her lip.

Dorothy lifted the lid of her desk and took out the sheet music she had been hiding inside. She walked stiffly to the front of the room and stood beside the piano to announce her number. Her heart beat so violently that only the thinnest whisper came out.

Never mind the words. She sat on the stool and opened the music. She took a deep breath to steady herself, curved her fingers and struck a chord: Da–DA!

Hoop–la!

The classroom door flew open and Uncle Max
leaped into the room. He looked splendid in high
boots and red pants and a loose embroidered tunic.
He beat a brief tattoo on the wooden floor with
the soles of his boots. Then, hands crossed on his
breast, he looked at Dorothy and waited for the
music to begin.

Instead of playing, Dorothy stood up. Her voice was small but clear as she said, "I asked my Uncle Max to show us how people in Russia like to dance when they feel happy. The dance is called a *gazotzka*. It looks easy but it isn't. I know, because I've tried." She sat down and started the music.

To the beat of the two-step, Uncle Max twirled and jumped and crouched on his knees as his legs flew this way and that. He finished in a burst of wild applause. Half the boys in the class rushed to surround Uncle Max and try to do the *gazotzka* too. The room shook with the thump of clapping heels and falling bodies.

Miss Cole stuck her head in the door and said crossly, "Mrs. Merrick, *please*! We must have better order here!"

Dorothy, standing near the piano, glanced shyly over toward Mama. Mama was fumbling in her bag for a handkerchief. Then she raised her head and Dorothy saw that her eyes were shining with tears. Over the top of the piano mother and daughter exchanged radiant smiles.

CHAPTER EIGHTEEN

Moving Day

It was moving day. The house was full of barrels and crates. The windows, bare of curtains, looked like staring eyes.

Daddy and Uncle Max and two hired movers were rapidly emptying the rooms of furniture and packaged belongings. They carried these things through the wide-open front door and stacked them into a rented van. "Portland Furniture Company" was lettered on the side of the truck. Alongside these words a fanciful red bird stood on one web-footed leg, balancing a bit of fluff on his enormous beak. "Easy Terms" said the words over the pelican's head, while the legend underneath him read "A Little Down On A Big Bill."

As Dorothy watched, the moving men stuffed the kitchen table into the truck, upside down on top of the piano. The table looked helpless with its legs stuck up in the air, like a beetle on its back. Next they hoisted the leather sofa into the van, and then some beds all broken apart. Mama's fern, tied with string around the top, waited at the curb with three barrels of dishes. Jumbled up this way, familiar objects looked ugly and sad.

"Where's Anabelle?" Dorothy asked as Uncle Max reeled past her with his arms around a heavy carton of books.

Max jerked his head toward the house. "Your mama brushes her hair."

Dorothy walked slowly up the path toward the front door. Her eyes traced the familiar figures made by cracks in the cement. Would the next girl who lived here be able to see those lovable bears and elephants and monkeys? Dorothy decided to leave a clue. She scraped up a handful of pebbles and set them carefully in all the right places. There! she thought, anybody can see that those are animals' eyes.

Then she remembered the hiding place under the porch. Would the next girl be lucky enough to find it? Dorothy noticed that Grandma was sitting on a porch rocker, her Hebrew bible in her lap. But it didn't matter any more if Dorothy's grown-ups learned about the secret place. Dorothy walked boldly over to the lattice and pulled it open an inch.

In the almost-empty kitchen, Anabelle sat on a high stool while Mama made curls in her red hair. Dorothy watched while Mama wetted a long strand and brushed it around and around her index finger. When Mama gently removed her finger she left a tight little corkscrew curl dangling by Anabelle's right ear.

Daddy passed through the kitchen, a lamp in each hand. "Oh, Jennie," he said. "We're almost ready to leave. Couldn't you just skip the curls for one day?"

"I will never let my girls leave the house looking like tramps," Mama replied.

Daddy sighed and went on out the door. "Here's Enid," he called back an instant later.

Dorothy ran outdoors to greet her friend. "I brought you a good-by gift," said Enid, handing Dorothy a small square package. She watched while Dorothy tore away the wrappings from a box of pink notepaper. "For you to write to me on. Let's write every day." Enid's dimples twinkled. "When there's anything secret we can use mirror writing."

"How can we write with a mirror?"

"That's not what I mean, silly." Enid ran to the road and smoothed out an area of the dust with the sole of her shoe. She found a stick and wrote: ⊃ И Ǝ Ⅎ "See?" she said. "That's 'Enid' backwards. Now you try."

Daddy hustled past. "Say goodby to Enid, Dorothy, and gather up your things. We're leaving."

Dorothy promised to write every day, and waved to Enid until her friend was out of sight. Then she walked slowly back into the house. She put her beaver hat on her head and snapped its elastic under her chin. She picked up Raggedy Ann, who had been waiting on the drainboard in the empty kitchen. On a sudden impulse, she ran upstairs to take a very last look around.

The girls' bedroom was deserted and sad. Dorothy opened the closet door and looked inside. Anabelle's toys were gone from the shelves, and there were no cheerful rows of clothes and heaps of shoes. The sun, shining in through the small window at the far end of the closet, made the house seem hollow. How cold it would look to the next girl who moved in. She might never know that Dorothy had lived here, and that this was a friendly house.

Dorothy decided to leave a message of welcome.

Gently she arranged Raggedy Ann in a sitting position on the closet floor. If she left the doll behind now, she realized, she would never see her again. Could she manage alone without Raggedy Ann's comfort for the rest of her life?

Dorothy studied Raggedy Ann's familiar painted mouth and shoe-button eyes. Raggedy Ann smiled steadfastly back. After a few moments, Dorothy closed the closet door and hurried out of the room.

ABOUT THE AUTHOR

Dorothy Nathan was born in Oregon and spent part of her childhood in a small town near Portland. She received her Bachelor of Arts degree from the University of California, and also holds a Master's degree in education. She has worked in a social agency and as a teacher, but in recent years has devoted most of her time to her family, and to writing. Her first book was *Women of Courage*.

Married to writer Paul Nathan and the mother of three children, Dorothy Nathan again lives in a small town, this time in New York State.

ABOUT THE ILLUSTRATOR

CAROLYN CATHER studied art history at Duke University, and later learned to draw while working for the newspaper *Stars and Stripes* in Japan after World War II.

She now lives in New York City, where she devotes her time to book illustration. She provided the illustrations for Dorothy Nathan's first book, *Women of Courage*.